RUN ZAN RUN

Also by Cathy MacPhail
Missing
Bad Company
Dark Waters
Fighting Back
Another Me
Underworld
Roxy's Baby
Worse Than Boys
Grass
Out of The Depths

The Nemesis Series
Into the Shadows
The Beast Within
Sinister Intent
Ride of Death

RUN ZAN RUN

CATHY MACPHAIL

BLOOMSBURY
LONDON OXFORD NEW YORK NEW DELHI SYDNEY

Bloomsbury Publishing, London, Oxford, New York, New Delhi and Sydney

Bloomsbury is a registered trademark of Bloomsbury Publishing Plc

Published in Great Britain in November 2001
by Bloomsbury Publishing Plc
50 Bedford Square, London WC1B 3DP

First published by Blackie in October 1994
Published by Puffin Books in January 1996

This edition published in 2011

A CIP catalogue record for this book is available from the British Library

ISBN 978 1 4088 1733 9

MIX
Paper from
responsible sources
FSC® C013604

Typeset by Dorchester Typesetting Group Ltd
Printed and bound in Great Britain by CPI Group (UK) Ltd, Croydon CR0 4YY

5 7 9 10 8 6 4

For my Katie

CHAPTER ONE

Katie trudged over the dump. This way at least she wouldn't meet Ivy Toner and her gang. It was the long road home from school, through the patch of waste ground where the city's tenements once stood. It was growing dusky in the late October afternoon. But Katie wasn't afraid. Not here. She was safer here, deserted though it was, than she'd be walking through the busy streets and lanes of the town.

Alone. She was so often alone nowadays. Her friends, one by one, had deserted her. Too afraid to be friendly in case they, merely by association with her, became the target for the bullying, the cruelty of Ivy Toner.

Katie kicked at a stone and looked around the dismal place. People dumped their rubbish here now. Black bags littered the area – cardboard boxes lay askew on the ground. A dump – a real dump – yet she was safer here.

She could feel the tears nip at her eyes, but she wouldn't cry.

Everyone told her one day Ivy Toner would grow tired of picking on her and move on to fresher, more fearing ground.

But when? It had been months since it began. Little things at first, almost comical at times. Pushing and jostling her in the corridors at school, not letting her pass. Chewing-gum on her seat in English. Katie had sat on it, and actually laughed back. Had that been her mistake? She had laughed when she should have fought.

But she wasn't aggressive. Didn't know how to be. She just wanted to be friends with everybody. Once, not so long ago, she had been everyone's favourite. Katie Cassidy, always with a smile on her face and something funny to say. Katie Cassidy, who used to make everyone laugh.

Everyone, except Ivy Toner. Perhaps that was what made her notice Katie, single her out for her special kind of attention.

And usually by Ivy's side were her two mates, Lindy Harkins and Michelle Thomson. But Katie didn't fear them. They didn't look her way unless Ivy was with them.

'You shouldn't show them that you're afraid,' her father had told her. 'Stand up to them. That's what these people don't understand. You'd have no more trouble.'

It was all right for him. He didn't have to go to school every day, alone. Never knowing when you were going to turn a corner and find them waiting for you.

They had trapped her in the girls' toilet one day. No one else there, except Ivy and her cronies . . . and Katie. She remembered the day bitterly, with shame. Ivy, trying to force her head down the toilet until Katie admitted, tears streaming down her face, that Ivy was a princess. Princess Ivy . . . and that she, Katie, was her slave.

She had run, crying, to the teacher, when they'd finally let her go. Though they had sworn the worst sort of vengeance if she ever told anyone about the incident. And that had only made things worse.

Ivy had denied any such involvement, providing witnesses to prove she was somewhere else at the time. Nevertheless, her reputation as a bully was well known, and she was given a final warning to leave Katie alone.

Now she did, mostly, but only at school. She was clever enough to know that the school could do nothing about what happened outside its jurisdiction.

Now she lay in wait for Katie as she walked home, as

she left school. And now, to make matters even worse, Katie was a 'grass' to be despised. Even others in the school turned from her, as if she was the one who had done something wrong.

She had never been so unhappy or alone in all her life.

She stamped the ground angrily and cried out. 'But I'm not even fourteen yet. It's not fair!'

And it wasn't. She didn't know how to handle all this. her teachers, her parents, her friends, none of them really understood what she was going through. None of them could do anything to help her.

She was alone.

Here on the dump she could cry and scream and vent her anger. There was no one to hear her. Here on the dump, she was safe.

At least, she had been until now.

'So this is where you've been getting to?'

Katie whirled around, wiping her tears with her sleeve as she did.

That voice chilled her. It was Ivy's.

There she stood, her dumpy bulk outlined against the grey sky, her lank black hair hanging over the collar of her jacket. Behind her, as always, Lindy and Michelle.

'Hidin' frae us, are you?'

Katie's throat went dry as she tried to speak. She felt clammy perspiration on her brow.

'I wish I wasn't so afraid,' she thought. If Ivy was ever alone she would at least try to fight her, but Ivy was never alone.

'You picked a nice quiet place anyway,' Ivy said, and the words sent another chill through Katie. Her eyes darted around her. Isolated, and deserted. What was it she had thought only a moment ago?

Here on the dump there was no one to hear her.

The realization of how alone she was made her gasp. The dump was no longer the safe haven it had once been. It never would be again.

Why had she come here? Katie took one step backwards. Ivy sneered. She looked all around the dump, lifted her hands and shrugged.

'There's no' anywhere you can hide here, hen.'

She took one menacing step towards her and Katie turned and ran.

'Get her!' Ivy screamed, and Lindy and Michelle began running too.

Katie darted one quick glance behind her. She'd never get away from them. There was nowhere to run, and when they caught her . . .

She let out a scream as she lost her footing, toppling down a bank of bin bags and rubbish and broken bits of furniture. She rolled over and over and finally landed at the bottom, sandwiched between the bags.

She could hear their voices, their footsteps thundering towards her. Any moment now, they would reach her. Any moment now, they would find her. She was done for.

Nothing could save her now.

Suddenly, a cardboard box nearby moved into life. All Katie could make out written on it were the words . . . Zan . . . Automatic Washing Machine. It was definitely moving.

Rats, thought Katie, there are rats here. As if Ivy wasn't enough. There were other rats here too. Only she wasn't so afraid of the four-legged kind.

And then, suddenly, out of the cardboard box, *she* emerged. As if by magic.

A girl, her hair almost the same colour as Katie's but without her healthy sheen. This girl's hair was matted, her face smudged with dirt. She was wearing a red shirt and trousers much too big for her . . . and a long overcoat. A man's overcoat.

Katie gasped. She heard the footsteps stop in mid-stride.

'Who the hell is that?' Ivy's voice.

'Is there a problem here?'

The girl's icy glance hadn't taken Katie in, but she was sure she knew she was there. She stepped from the box as she spoke.

'Buzz off,' she said.

'Ha!' Ivy sneered. 'You gonny make me?'

The girl shrugged. 'If that's what you want.'

Katie couldn't make out her accent. It wasn't Scottish, and yet it had a distinctive burr in it that couldn't be anything else.

Who was this girl?

Ivy was still laughing. She wasn't afraid, of course. She had Lindy and Michelle. One against three, the kind of odds Ivy liked.

Yet the girl didn't look afraid either. Maybe she was too stupid to be afraid. She stepped forward, oozing menace.

'Piss off.'

Katie sank deeper into her hole. If the worst came to the worst, she would have to step out and help this girl. And saying 'Piss off' to Ivy and her gang wasn't going to help them when they were pleading for mercy.

'You really are goin' to try to take us?'

Lindy and Michelle were laughing too. The girl stopped her advance.

'I won't have to try too hard with you three wimps.'

She moved closer to them, out of Katie's line of vision. Katie braced herself to stand up. To go to her aid. Yet she couldn't move. Maybe this was her chance to run away, while they were busy mollecating the girl. She was probably as bad as they were anyway. She might have mugged her if they hadn't been there. Why should she help? It wasn't as if this girl was defending her.

She heard a thump and a groan. The battle had begun. A scream.

'Let go!'

She couldn't make out the voice. She wanted to peek over the top of the bin bags to see what was happening but she was too afraid. The least she could do, she decided, was to stay here and make sure the girl was all right when they were finished with her. Administer first aid, or even the kiss of life.

'Come back here, you two!'

Ivy's voice broke into her thoughts. Feet were pounding away. Two sets of them.

Lindy and Michelle!

'Seems you're on your own. It's just you and me.'

There was another thump and another scream. A definite Ivy type scream. 'You fight dirty.'

Ivy was accusing someone else of fighting dirty? What was happening over there?

'I'll get you another day . . . that's a promise.'

And Ivy was running away. It was unbelievable.

The girl began to laugh. Her laughter echoed eerily around the darkening dump.

Katie held her breath, more afraid than ever now. If she could do that to Ivy . . . what was she going to do to Katie?

'And you . . . hiding down there . . . don't you come back here either!' The voice was threatening.

Katie waited, expecting every second that she would be dragged over the bin bags and get the same treatment as Ivy. She waited, but nothing happened. Finally, taking a deep breath, Katie emerged from her hiding place.

The girl had gone. Katie looked all around. The dump was deserted again. And yet she had the strange feeling that somewhere, someone was watching her every move. She took one last look around. Then she ran.

At home that night she couldn't stop thinking about the strange girl on the dump. Who was she? And had it really happened at all? The whole incident didn't seem real somehow.

It all came back to her in her dreams. Ivy and Lindy and Michelle, confronting her on the dump. She was alone. The dump was deserted. But the girl would come. Katie wasn't afraid. She started to run, but she couldn't move. Ivy was closing in on her. She was going to catch her, and suddenly she knew this time no girl would come to her rescue. Ivy racing nearer and nearer. Ivy at her heels. Ivy with her fingers gripping tight on her hair. Ivy had her!

Katie awoke in a cold sweat. That's what would have happened if the girl hadn't appeared.

And she hadn't even thanked her!

'Don't you come back here either!' the girl had said. But she would go back to the dump. On the way to school. She had to. She had to see if this girl was still there. And if she was . . . well, she was going to thank her now.

In the crisp early morning air, the dump looked different. The sun shone on the shiny black bin bags and made them look almost picturesque. Katie stood for a moment and looked around. There was no one here.

The girl had gone . . . if she'd ever been here in the first place. Katie was beginning to think she had imagined the whole thing.

This was silly. Useless. But she knew she had to try. She took a deep breath.

'If you're here . . . ' Her voice sounded peculiar, bellowing out into the silence. 'The girl who helped me yesterday . . . I just wanted to say . . . Thank you.'

She waited for some kind of reaction. Nothing. Not a movement.

Oh well, at least she had tried. Katie turned to go, and just then, suddenly, from nowhere, came a voice, the voice from yesterday.

'I told you not to come back!'

Katie almost fainted. Where had the voice come from? There was no one here. Not a soul. Then, from a cardboard box that looked as if it had been slung carelessly against a half demolished wall, *she* rose. She looked more than a little annoyed. What am I doing here? Katie thought. What is she going to do to *me* now? She's probably every bit as bad as Ivy!

'I . . . I . . . I . . . ' Katie could hardly get a word out. 'I just wanted to thank you for yesterday.'

'I was trying to have a lie in.' The girl drew a hand

through her tousled hair. 'Anyway. Thank me for what?'

Katie forced herself to take a step forward. 'For yesterday. Remember? You helped me.'

Her answer was almost a snarl. 'Helped you! I don't help anybody. I got rid of them because this is my place!' She gestured around the dump. As far as Katie was concerned she could have it. 'I tried to get rid of you too if I remember right. But you're kind of dumb, aren't you?'

'Well, you might not have meant to help me, but those girls have been giving me such a lot of bother. I don't know what they would have done if you hadn't stepped in when you did.'

The girl stepped from the box and brushed herself down, all the time eyeing Katie curiously. 'What on earth are you frightened of them for? They're wimps.'

'Wimps?' Katie took another tentative step forward, amazed. 'Ivy . . . the last girl to run away, she's the toughest girl in our school. Even the boys are frightened of her.'

'What do you mean, *even* the boys? You must have a school full of wimps.'

She had every right to think that. Especially after the way Katie had hidden. 'I was coming to help you yesterday. Honest.'

The girl shrugged that aside.

'Didn't need any help. Is that why you come this way? To avoid Bootface?'

Katie giggled. Bootface Ivy. She liked the sound of that.

'You've seen me?'

The girl nodded. 'Every day.'

'Why have I never seen you?'

'I'm an expert at hiding.' She suddenly began to laugh. And Katie noticed, for the first time, her eyes. Bright blue, almost mischievous eyes. 'You talk to yourself. I've heard you.'

Katie blushed.

'Don't worry about it.' The girl punched her arm. 'I thought I was the only one who did that.'

'What are you doing on the dump anyway?'

'I live here.'

Katie looked around. There wasn't a building, a structure of any kind. 'Here?' She repeated. 'Where?'

The girl stepped over to the cardboard box. 'It's called a mobile home.'

'You're kidding me on. Nobody lives in a cardboard box.'

'Don't they?'

'But what about your home, your mum and dad?'

Her eyes lost their sparkle . . . or had the sun gone in? Katie couldn't be sure.

'Not got any. Look, I'm moving on. It's getting a bit too busy for my liking around here.' She hesitated. 'I wouldn't worry about Bootface too much. She's a nothing.'

Katie stood watching her walk away, carrying her home with her. Did people really live like that? On the dumps? She knew there were homeless people. Wasn't her dad always on about their duty to them? But as young as . . .

She realized with dismay she didn't even know her name.

'Hey?' She called out and the girl turned round. 'My name's Katie Cassidy, by the way. You never told me your name.'

She stood for a moment, her head cocked to one side, reminding Katie of a bird. Then she smiled. 'I don't tell anybody my name.' She said it as if having a name didn't matter. 'Call me anything you want.'

As the girl turned again, Katie caught sight of the faded print on the box she carried. Zan.

'That's what I'll call her,' she thought. 'I'll call her Zan.'

She'd probably never see her again anyway, this strange, mysterious girl. But as Katie watched her go, she was glad she'd met her. Glad too that she'd come back this morning to thank her.

Ivy Toner could be beaten, could be frightened.

She'd never be afraid of her again.

Thanks to the girl in the cardboard box.

CHAPTER TWO

Katie was in the corridor waiting to go into her history class when Ivy turned the corner and began striding towards her, menace in every step.

She could feel her heart begin to pound, could sense the other girls turning from her, as they always did, too afraid of antagonizing Ivy to show any friendship towards her.

Ivy stopped beside her, flanked as ever by Michelle and Lindy.

'So, where's your clatty friend now?'

'She fairly scared the knickers off you anyway.' That was what she wanted to say . . . instead, she swallowed.

Ivy poked at her. 'I asked you a question.'

'She . . . she's not a friend of mine . . . ' She heard herself answer. She should be sticking up for Zan. Yet here she was, ready to desert the girl in the cardboard box to appease Ivy.

'You jist tell her to stay well away from me.'

Ivy curled her lip and tried to look fierce. Katie had a sudden picture of her fleeing over the dump. She giggled.

'I know,' she said, madness sweeping over her. 'She fights dirty.'

Ivy almost fainted. To tell the truth, so did Katie. Had she a death wish, or something? Ivy knew what Katie was laughing at, what she was referring to. She knew that Katie had seen her running away. That memory made Ivy madder than ever. She leaned very close to Katie's mouth. Katie shrank back so she wouldn't have to smell her stale smoky breath.

'I'm goin' to get you, hear me? No' now. No' today. No' here. But I'll get you.' She stood straight, still sneering. 'A' right, Katie?'

She laughed as she was leaving her. So did Michelle and Lindy. Katie felt the cold beads of sweat form on her brow. She had no doubt Ivy meant what she said. She would get her.

Now what was she going to do?

'Aren't you hungry?' Her mother lifted the untouched plate from the table.

Katie shrugged.

'Is something bothering you, Katie?' Her mother sat across from her. She was very pretty, with large dark eyes and a head of rich dark curls. She looked much younger than her forty-four years. She was a little bit of a snob, but she had a kind heart and at least once a day did something completely silly.

Katie longed to tell her. But she knew what would happen if she did. Exactly what had happened before. Her mother would insist she be taken out of that 'rough school'. Her father would insist with equal fervour that she remain where she was and face up to the bullies. 'That's the only way to beat them.'

They would have an awful row about her, and the last thing she wanted was for them to fight.

Her mother, however, guessed at the problem. 'Is it that girl? Is she still giving you bother?'

Katie tried to protest, but too weakly.

'She is! I knew it! Douglas!' She pulled her husband's paper from his fingers with a flourish. 'I want her out of that school immediately!'

Her father looked from one hand to the other, wondering where his paper had gone to. Then his eyes moved to his wife, standing over him.

'Katherine! I was reading the news.'

'We have something much more important to discuss. Our daughter. I want her out of that school.'

Her father sighed. 'Now will you give Katie credit for standing on her own two feet. She's not going to give in to any bullies, are you honey?'

Slowly, Katie shook her head.

'You see?'

'You'd be much happier in another school, wouldn't you dear?'

Again, Katie nodded.

'There!'

'She's only saying that to agree with you.'

'And she's only staying in that school so she won't hurt your feelings.'

'And all you want to do is get her into Riverside Academy.'

'It's a fine school. It was my school too. If my mother knew I'd let her granddaughter go to that rough school . . . why, she'd turn in her grave.'

'Katherine! You know fine and well your mother is alive and fighting fit and living in Aberdeen.'

'Well,' Katie's mother said, refusing as usual to be beaten, 'if she was dead she'd be birling in her grave.'

Katie stood up. 'Honestly, Mum, I'm fine, I really am.' She looked from one to the other, trying to convince them. 'In fact, I think she's going to leave me alone from now on.'

It seemed almost as if that might be true. Ivy and her cohorts ignored her in the corridors at school, swishing past her as if she didn't exist. No longer did they wait for her outside the school gates either.

So why did she feel they were only biding their time?

Katie still walked over the dump, almost without fear – there was never any sign of Ivy.

There was never any sign of Zan, either – she couldn't help but call her that – every cardboard box she knocked on was empty. Yet Katie longed to see her again, and tell her it was all over, thanks to her.

At least, she thought it was all over.

Hallowe'en came along, and there was a disco at the school. Many of the pupils were dressing up for it, but not Katie. She decided she'd feel silly walking up to school alone, dressed up. And she would be alone. Her so-called friends were still too afraid of Ivy to risk calling for her.

Her parents were having a fancy dress party of their

own, and the house was decorated with masks and sticky buns hanging from string and apples bobbing in buckets of water for the fun and games they intended for their friends.

'I'll run you up to school,' her mother offered. She was half dressed as Cleopatra, with her make-up completed and wearing her wig, but otherwise incongruously attired in a jogging suit.

'No, Mum, honestly, I'm meeting some of the girls.' She lied because her mother would have insisted if she hadn't. And it would be so embarrassing to be driven up to school with her dressed like that!

Her father, a convincing Count Dracula, would be an even more embarrassing chauffeur, and there were people in school who already thought her parents rather strange.

'Now, are you sure?' her mother asked again.

'Honest, I'm meeting them round the corner.'

It was already dark when she left, but the road was brightly lit and busy, especially tonight, Hallowe'en, and it was fun being out in the street. Guisers of all shapes and sizes passed her, in all sorts of colourful and imaginative costumes.

She wished now she had taken the trouble to dress up.

Only at the old bridge spanning the disused railway track did the road become quiet. No guisers here, no children. Only an eerie quiet.

Ominous.

Katie began to hurry, the clipping of her shoes the only echoing sound as she almost ran across the bridge. She was nearly there. A car passed along the high road, its lights bright and welcoming. Safety.

Out of nowhere Ivy sprang. She had been hiding behind the wall. Behind her Michelle, then Lindy, till all three stood threateningly in front of her.

Katie glanced around. The street was empty.

Fight back, a voice inside told her. Kick, shout. scream. Do anything, but get away.

'I don't want any trouble.' She knew her voice was trembling.

Ivy sniggered. 'You're no' goin' to give us any.' She nodded to Lindy and Michelle. 'Get her!'

Before she could move, a hand was clamped over Katie's mouth, her shoulders firmly gripped. Lindy and Michelle lifted her off the ground, and half carried, half dragged her after Ivy. Round the wall of the bridge, through open fencing and bushes. She felt nettles sting her face as they pulled her roughly along beside the wall, with the sheer rock drop under them on to the tracks below.

Ivy turned on her. 'I told you I'd get you. Didn't I? Well,' her next words sent shivers through Katie, 'tonight's the night.' She nodded to the other two. 'Get her up there.'

'Up there' was a brick wall built to break a fall on to the rocks and tracks below.

Katie screamed, and knew it was useless. Who would hear her? Who'd take notice of a scream on Hallowe'en?

Katie was pushed on to the wall. Standing there, looking down – she couldn't stop herself – she had never been so afraid in her life. She began to sway and tried to step back. Ivy's hand gripped her calves. 'No way, hen,' she said. 'You take a good look. 'Cause that's where you're goin'.'

Katie gasped. She couldn't be serious. Even Ivy Toner couldn't be that bad.

Ivy began to shake her legs.

'Ivy, don't!' This was Lindy. Even she didn't think Ivy'd go that far. 'We could get into trouble for this.'

No worry about Katie's safety, only their own.

'Aye, let her go,' Michelle pleaded. But Ivy's grip remained firm.

Katie was afraid to breathe, afraid even the slightest movement would send her tumbling on to the rocks below.

'Are ye ready?' Katie could feel the pressure on her legs. One more push, no matter how gentle, and she'd be over.

She was going to die. At that moment, she had no doubt of that. She was about to die.

'*Aiee!*' The sudden shriek was from Lindy, standing on Ivy's right. Katie was too afraid to glance round. She could only concentrate on keeping her balance – on not falling.

'Hey, Lindy. Where ur you?'

There was no answer to Ivy's question, but her grip remained as firm as ever.

'*Aiee!*' Now it was Michelle's scream that made Ivy jump. Startling her so much that Katie almost fell. What was happening? She didn't dare look back to see.

'Michelle?' Ivy sounded scared. 'Lindy!'

But there was no answer. Lindy and Michelle had vanished.

'Who's there?' As Ivy turned to confront whoever it was she let go of Katie. Katie didn't waste a second. She jumped back off the wall, on to safe ground, just glad to be alive, glad to be staying alive. She fell badly. Her ankle exploded with pain and she grasped it and rolled further away from Ivy, out of sight. From the shadows she watched Ivy. She was jumping around, looking left, looking right, her eyes wide and afraid.

'Lindy! Michelle!'

'They can't help you now.'

The girl stepped from the darkness. Zan. Her face dirty and her hair matted, but her eyes bright and challenging.

'You again . . .' Ivy's voice trembled. She was afraid. Ivy Toner was afraid! 'Where are my mates?'

Zan only smiled. That seemed to scare Ivy even more.

'Let me go.'

'Who's stopping you?'

Ivy darted to the left and the right, her nervous eyes never leaving Zan. Suddenly she rushed at her, trying to take her by surprise. Zan sidestepped her neatly, put out her foot, and tripped her over. Ivy crashed to the rocky ground, falling heavily, and Katie heard her howl with pain.

Zan placed a foot on Ivy's back.

'Let me up!' Ivy screamed.

'I'll let you up . . . but only if you promise never to touch, go near, or threaten my wee friend again.'

'Let me up!' Ivy screamed.

Zan pushed Ivy's face closer to the ground. 'What are you not going to do?' she insisted.

Katie gasped as she saw Ivy reach out her hand to grab Zan's ankle. If she did she could topple her. But Zan was too quick. Suddenly, she was sitting astride Ivy's back, both her wrists clamped in one dirty, strong little hand. With the other she pressed Ivy's face into the dirt. 'What are you not going to do?' she repeated.

There were almost tears in Ivy's voice as she answered. 'I'm . . . not . . . goin' to . . . touch her . . . again—'

'Her?'

'Your . . . friend . . . Katie—'

'And what else?'

'Or go near her . . . or threaten her . . . or anythin' else. Just let me up!'

With one bound Zan was on her feet, pulling Ivy up after her. 'Get goin', and just remember this. If you don't keep that promise, I'll come after you. And you don't know when I might pop up. So watch it!'

She threw Ivy away from her.

Ivy ran, stumbling, falling more than once, pulling herself up the embankment to the road once more. Then she disappeared into the night.

Katie stood up and winced as she put weight on her ankle.

Zan turned at the sound. She smiled. 'You'll never learn, will you? Letting people like that get the better of you. Ankle sore?'

'Who are you?' was all Katie could ask.

Zan shrugged. 'Nobody. I don't know. Does it matter?'

'You told her I was your friend.'

'I suppose you are. Never had one before?'

Katie tried to step towards her and winced again.

'Here, lean on me,' Zan said, slipping an arm around Katie's waist and holding the hand that Katie draped around her shoulders.

'I thought I was going to die. I don't know how I'll ever thank you.'

'You don't have to . . . but do me a favour.'

'What?'

'Learn some self-defence, judo or something. Learn to take care of yourself.'

'Where did you learn to fight?'

Zan laughed. 'It was either fight back, or don't survive. I fought back.'

'How did you find me here?'

'You found me. I moved house. Under the bridge. Thought it would be quieter.'

They climbed back on to the road. There was no sign of Ivy.

'You know, you've got to stand up to people like that. Bullies thrive on fear.'

'I don't suppose you've ever been afraid of anyone in your life.'

She felt Zan tense beside her. 'I've been afraid . . . ' she said softly.

When they reached Katie's house Zan released her. 'There. You can go in yourself.'

'Aren't you coming with me? My mum and dad will want to thank you.'

Zan held back, looking at the house. How inviting it must seem to her, Katie thought. The warm glow of the lamps lighting the windows, the hall lit up and the red carpeted stairs rising to the floor above. There were sounds too, music and laughter. Her parents' party in full progress. Katie wanted her to come in so much.

She clasped her hand. 'Come with me. Stay with me, the night at least. Sleep in a warm bed. You'd love my mum and dad.'

The light, the smile vanished from her eyes. 'Never!'

She snapped the words out. 'I'm safer where I am!'

And suddenly she was running down the street, away from Katie, away from warmth and security. Running back to her cardboard box.

CHAPTER THREE

'What do you mean? A girl in a cardboard box?' Her father had taken out his false fangs, but still managed to look slightly ridiculous with his slicked-back black hair and white face. Katie was finding it very difficult not to giggle. There was a sea of made-up faces listening to her story, and a penguin examining her ankle.

'Honestly, Dad. She does. She lives in a cardboard box. She helped me, the other day . . . and again tonight.'

'It's only a bad sprain, I think. Better have it X-rayed anyway to be on the safe side,' the penguin said seriously.

'Lucky you were at the party, Dr Robb,' her father said.

Katie giggled.

'Are you joking about this, Katie?' her mother warned her. She looked around the room. 'Girls living in cardboard boxes, here, in this town? I can hardly believe it.'

'It's true,' Katie protested.

'You're always hearing about homeless children,' her father went on, 'but you think of them in London, in New York, not in your own home town.'

A woman dressed as Adolf Hitler patted her head and said gently, 'The poor little mite, she's come through such a lot tonight.'

Katie giggled again, and she could tell by her mother's narrowed eyes that she was doing her credibility no good at all.

'If you're lying Katie . . . '

'Honest, Mum . . . '

'It's nerves making her giggle, Katherine,' the penguin said. 'She's had a shock . . . '

'Maybe we should get the police. Girls doing a thing like that, they deserve to be charged.'

Katie protested immediately. 'No, please, Mum. Ivy Toner has had a big enough fright for one night. I don't think she'll give me any more trouble.'

The memory still pleased her. Ivy beaten, Ivy afraid, running.

'What was this girl's name?'

Katie almost said Zan – but stopped as she realized how stupid it sounded.

Her hesitation made her mother even more suspicious. 'I . . . I don't know.'

Her mother bent down beside her. Lovely as usual, especially now, looking exactly like Cleopatra. She blinked startled black eyes at her. 'You mean this girl helped you, helped you twice and you didn't even ask her name?'

'She wouldn't tell me . . . ' She looked around at all the questioning, wondering faces. 'She's been living like that for months, and she's only my age.' There was a shocked, communal gasp.

'I'm going to have to do something about this,' her father said, and Katie knew when she heard that kind of determination in his voice nothing would stop him. He was a well-respected local councillor, who had a reputation for helping the people who most needed help.

'Well, you can do what you want for the homeless, Douglas. But right now, I'm taking my daughter to hospital.'

'I'll be all right, Mum. I don't want to spoil your party.'

Cleopatra kissed her cheek. 'You could never do that, never. You're the priority here.'

Poor Zan, Katie thought, as her mother slid an arm round her tenderly and helped her from the couch.

Never to be anyone's priority. Never to know the security of sleeping safe and warm.

'Are you coming?' Her mother already had the car keys in her hand.

'Looking like this?' Her father held out his scarlet-lined cloak and looked even more like Dracula.

'It's Hallowe'en,' her mother said, sensibly. 'You won't look the least bit unusual.'

'And they took you to hospital dressed up?'

Her friends, those friends who only last week had refused to speak to her, were now gathered round listening to her story, eager for every detail. News of Ivy's humiliation had raced round the school, just as news of an under-age girl living rough on the dump had raced round the town. Ivy wasn't at school. Lindy and Michelle were, but they were only cyphers without their leader.

'Yes . . . ' Katie giggled at the memory. Her parents had caused quite a stir in casualty, especially as her mother remained in her regal character throughout the visit and almost had the doctors curtseying in front of her. As for her father, he had to suffer the wisecracks from the drunks who were also being treated in casualty.

'In for a wee transfusion, are ye, Drac?'

'Have you come for a takeaway meal, Count?' Then the drunk indicated his neck. 'Here, Count, have a drink on me.'

'No, thank you,' her father had retorted. 'I think I'd rather have my fangs drilled . . . without anaesthetic.'

She loved her parents. They were so funny.

'And is it true, Katie? Did this girl beat Ivy?'

'Yes, this one girl.' She looked round at them all. At some time each of them had been Ivy's victim. 'She says we shouldn't be afraid of her. Ivy was frightened. Really frightened. I saw her run off, scared stiff. Bullies thrive on the fear we show them. That's what Zan says.'

'Zan?'

'That's what I call her.'

'She's really mysterious, isn't she?'

'I suppose she is.'

Katie became something of a celebrity in the school, bathing in Zan's reflected glory. She was always careful, though, to point out that she had done nothing. Everything was due to Zan.

It was two days before Ivy returned to school. A different Ivy. A quiet, subdued Ivy. One who didn't even look Katie's way in the corridors.

As for Zan, searches were proving futile. Her father was trying hard not to be disheartened. 'Where can she be? I have whole groups of volunteers out searching for her.'

'She's good at hiding,' Katie told him. 'She said so.'

'But why should she hide? We mean her no harm. We only want to help.'

Maybe, a voice inside whispered to Katie (where did it come from?), maybe she didn't want to be helped.

It was Saturday morning and Katie was hurrying to the sports centre. She was late for badminton, so she took a short cut through back closes and back greens. Suddenly a hand grabbed her and pulled her against the wall of an old disused wash-house.

Ivy! She was in Ivy's clutches again!

'What the hell do you think you've done!'

Katie opened her eyes. Zan!

'What have I done?'

'You told them about me. You told everybody about me.'

Katie swallowed. This was the Zan she had first encountered. Defensive and aggressive. There was nothing friendly about this Zan. 'I'm sorry. I didn't know I wasn't supposed to. But they don't mean you any harm, Zan. They want to help.'

'I know, and I know how they want to help. Put me in a home, look for my real parents, send me back. NEVER!'

She screamed the last word out and Katie was almost frightened. She looked into her eyes and realized it was Zan who was frightened. 'Why did you run away from home, Zan?'

Zan was breathing hard. For a time, Katie thought she wasn't going to answer her. Finally, she said, 'Don't ever ask me that. Ever.'

What could have happened? Katie thought. What terrible thing could have happened to her?

'They're everywhere,' Zan went on breathlessly. 'Police, social workers, do-gooders. I wanted to stay here for a while. I like this town, it's big enough to hide in, but not to get lost in . . . and this is how you thank me.'

'I'm sorry. But . . . what can I do?'

'Nothing.'

'I'd undo it if I could. Honest.'

Zan leaned up against the wall thoughtfully. All at once, her eyes brightened again. 'Maybe you can.'

'How?'

'Tell them you were lying . . . tell them I don't exist.'

'But why should I have lied?'

Zan shrugged. 'You were afraid you'd get into trouble for fighting. I don't know. Think of something.'

'But they'd never believe me.' Yet even as she said it she remembered their incredulous faces, her mother's especially, and knew they'd believe her all too readily.

What she was really afraid of was what her parents would say. Lying, wasting police time . . . Maybe she'd end up in borstal, with a hundred other Ivys.

She looked at Zan. For the first time, she didn't look tough, or defiant. She looked vulnerable. 'I just want things the way they were. I want to stay the way I am.'

Zan had helped her when she needed it most. The only one who had. Now it was Katie's turn.

'I'll tell them. I'll make them believe me. Honest I will.'

Zan's face lit up. 'That's all I wanted to hear.' She began to hurry away. 'You promise?'

'I promise.'

'See you, Katie, you're a real friend.'

'So are you, Zan.'

They smiled at each other and then Zan was gone, dodging through the back closes and away.

'I hope she comes to visit me in prison,' Katie thought, trudging home. Forgetting about badminton. Better get it over with now.

'What do you mean, she doesn't exist?' Her father still hadn't got over the shock of her admission.

'How many times does she have to tell you, Douglas?'

'But I've just started a campaign, in conjunction with the local paper, to save homeless people in the town.'

'They're still there,' Katie tried to comfort him. 'It's just that she's not one of them.'

'You've made me look like a right idiot. Do you know that, Katie?'

Her mother had taken the news better. She had never fully believed Katie's story. She took her hand now.

'So you're saying that you fought Ivy Toner, and these other girls, singlehanded.'

It didn't sound too believable to Katie either. 'Yes . . .' she said weakly.

'My little Katie?'

'I'd just had enough with Ivy, Mum. I blew up. I don't know where I got the strength to do it.'

'I'm about to blow up too,' Katie's father retorted. 'I'll have to let the police know, the papers . . . I'm going to look like a complete fool.'

Her mother turned on him. 'Is that all that's bothering you? If Katie got rid of the bully by her own efforts, I'm very proud of her. And so should you be.' She looked again at her daughter. 'You are telling the truth this time, aren't you?'

Katie had never deliberately lied to her mother, not over something as serious as this. It was the hardest thing she had ever done, harder even than facing up to Ivy Toner every day in school.

'It's the truth, Mum. This other girl just doesn't exist.'

It was the same at school.

'But Ivy Toner saw her,' her friends all pointed out. 'She says you're lying.'

Now that was going to be a problem. 'She's mistaken,' Katie assured them, she hoped with conviction.

'Why did you lie?'

'I have my reasons.' They had all asked the same questions. She always gave the same, enigmatic answers. She just hoped no one would ask what those reasons were.

Ivy, however, didn't say too much about the news that Zan didn't exist. She knew different, of course. It wasn't until one day, in the school toilets, that Katie discovered why she'd been so quiet.

She was just about to come out of one of the cubicles when she heard Lindy and Michelle's voices, as they came into the toilets.

'She's sayin' that lassie doesn't even exist.'

'I know,' Michelle answered. 'How can she say that, Ivy?'

Katie froze. Ivy was there too.

'We know she does. We saw her.'

'I know . . . but . . .'

'But what, Michelle?'

'Well, Ivy . . . Me and Lindy were just thinkin' . . .'

'That makes a change.'

Lindy laughed stupidly. 'But you know we never actually saw them together . . . at the same time . . .'

Michelle spoke up. 'Together like . . .'

'What is it you two are tryin' to say?'

Lindy took a deep breath. 'That first time Katie ran away, at the dump. Remember, she disappeared, she fell. Then this other yin just kind of . . . appears, out of a cardboard box.'

'I mean, it was dead funny. Did you no' think so yourself, Ivy?'

'Was it heck!'

Michelle went on, her voice hesitant. 'Then that second time, at the bridge. Katie was standing there . . . you had hold of her legs, so where did this other yin come from, Ivy? . . . And . . . where did Katie go? She jumped off the wall and then . . . she was away . . . and we couldn't see her . . . '

'The other one had grabbed you when she was still on the wall, remember, stupid?'

'I don't know, Ivy.' Michelle's voice was nervous. 'One minute I was watching her, the next I was flat on my back. I couldn't say for sure what happened. I was pure dead frightened.'

'I never saw anything either.' This was Lindy. 'I just know I don't know where Katie went, either time.'

'Aye, you were too busy running.'

Both girls protested now. 'But honest, Ivy . . . D'ye no' think . . . '

'Think what?' Ivy sneered. 'What is it you two are tryin' to say?'

Katie could picture their faces. And she thought she understood what it was they were trying to say. But it was unbelievable. It was all unbelievable. How could they think such a thing?

47

'They're the same person . . . Katie . . . and this other one. They've got to be!'

'What? You think she runs into a cardboard box and does a quick change . . . you've been watching too many Superman videos!'

It was Michelle's turn to put in her tuppence worth. 'But she said she didn't exist . . . and we never saw them thegether . . . I don't know, Ivy . . . I'm scared.'

'You're talkin' a load of codswallop!'

'How do you explain it then . . .?' Lindy's voice was almost hysterical. 'How did this other lassie know when Katie was in trouble? How was she always there exactly when she needed her?'

'You don't really believe all this?'

Their silence proved they did.

'They're different, I tell you!' But Ivy's voice wavered as she said it. Did she perhaps wonder too?

Katie chose that as her moment to step from the cubicle. Her sudden presence took them all by surprise.

She wanted to rush out, but forced herself to run her hands slowly under the tap, and just as deliberately dry them. They were unnerved by her behaviour, she could tell. For once, they were afraid of her.

'Talking about me, were you?'

She looked from Lindy to Michelle, completely ignoring Ivy. What was it in her eyes that made them suddenly need to rush to a class?

'Got to go, Ivy.'

'See you, Ivy.'

Then she and Ivy Toner were alone. For a long moment neither of them said a word.

'I know that other yin exists. I don't think there's anythin' magic about you.'

Katie didn't answer. She just continued to stare at Ivy, forced herself to. For Zan's sake she had to.

'Are you sure?' she heard herself say, and the voice didn't sound like Katie's voice at all. It sounded like Zan's.

'I'll prove she does. I don't care how long it takes. One of these days, I'll prove it.'

And as Katie listened to her heels echoing down the corridors she knew Ivy Toner wouldn't rest until she had.

CHAPTER FOUR

Katie lay in bed that night thinking over all that had happened. Only a few weeks go she had been afraid, constantly afraid. Now it was as if a weight had been lifted from her. Oh, there was still Ivy to deal with. Ivy would never let go till she knew the truth, but she pushed Ivy and her threats from her mind, just for tonight. She snuggled further under the duvet and cuddled Barney Bear against her. Tonight she was cosy, and warm, and safe.

And, suddenly, she had a picture of Zan somewhere in the town. Alone, sleeping in a cold and draughty cardboard box. She had no Barney Bear to snuggle up with. Probably never had. And she could never sleep contented. There would always be dangers.

Katie looked around her room, with its bright yellow walls, and the posters of her favourite pop groups stuck up everywhere. Signs of home. She was so lucky. Zan had made her realize just how lucky she was to have a home, and a mother and a father who loved her.

Yet Zan didn't seem to envy her. In fact, remembering the wary, frightened look in her eyes when Katie mentioned staying the night, Zan was more afraid of a night in a normal home than she was of sleeping in a cardboard box.

What was Zan's secret? What terrible thing had happened to make her run away?

Katie stretched and yawned and began to dream . . .

Perhaps Zan was a princess . . . the only survivor of her royal family. Assassins had been sent out to find her, to eliminate her . . . that was why she had to hide, why her identity had to remain a secret.

Or perhaps she was a spy. She had learned a secret formula that could destroy the world. The end of civilization as we know it, and all that . . . Yes, that would account for everything. She could trust no one. She would have to remain a fugitive for ever . . . Good old Zan. Well, she could depend on Katie. She would hide her identity. Ivy Toner would never find out the truth, no matter what devious methods she used.

All Katie's troubles were over, thanks to Zan. Life was wonderful again . . .

And like the optimist she was, she drifted off into deep, contented sleep.

All her troubles were over! She knew how foolish that idea had been as soon as she stepped into the playground next morning.

'There she is!' Katie looked across at the army of schoolboys who were advancing toward her and realized that the 'she' they were referring to was none other than herself.

'Come on! How did you do it?' This came from the smallest of the boys, a first-year with tousled blond hair and a cheeky face.

'How did I do what?'

'Oh, come on, Katie, you know . . .' This boy was taller. Mark something or other, she seemed to remember. 'How did you manage to fight off Big Ivy and her mates?'

It wasn't me, she almost said, but she bit her lip just in time.

'Lindy said you turned into this other lassie . . . Is that right, Katie? Did you?'

'Changed right in front o' them . . . she said that.'

The questions were being fired at her from all directions.

'Are you magic?' This finally, was the small boy again, eager for an answer.

They were all quiet suddenly, all waiting for the same answer.

'Of course I'm not magic,' Katie said at last. 'I fought off Ivy Toner and her mates. They've got to say that so they don't look stupid.'

'But how, Katie? I mean . . . look at the size of you.'

Pint-sized, her father called her, and liable to stay that way.

'It's not size that counts,' she told them.

'You never liked fightin' before.'

'And I don't like fighting now. But when you've got no other choice you have to stand up for yourself.'

She could see more in the playground joining the group gathered round her, hanging on her every word. She'd never had so much attention.

'How did you fight her?'

'Aye, tell us, Katie.' The little blond boy pulled at her blazer. 'I'm aye gettin' picked on by the big boys, Katie. I don't know how to fight.'

'I think we all should learn some kind of self-defence. Learn to protect ourselves.' She was remembering what Zan had said. 'Bullies thrive on fear. And we shouldn't

53

desert someone who's being bullied either. That's what we do, because we're afraid. If we all stand together, bullies can't harm us.'

Her father would have been proud of her. She had heard him making speeches just like that.

Unfortunately, it wasn't what her audience wanted to hear.

'But how did you fight them, Katie?'

'Did you punch them, Katie?'

'Did you kick them?'

She tried hard to remember exactly what Zan had done. She put down her school bag to demonstrate. 'I kind of tripped them up . . . and . . . I kind of jumped to the side like this . . . and . . .'

The little blond started miming karate kicks and punches and the crowd roared with laughter. 'You mean like this, *Haaaayaaa*!' His scream alone would have frightened the life out of anyone.

'Katie Cassidy!' The voice shrieked out behind Katie, and her audience scattered in all directions.

Katie whirled round to face an irate Miss Withers, the head maths teacher. 'What do you think you're doing!' she shrieked again.

Katie opened her mouth to speak but Miss Withers

didn't wait for an answer. 'Come with me! Thisss . . .' she hissed the word out, 'is going to be continued without an audience!'

As Katie hurried into the school and along the corridors behind a clattering Miss Withers, she wondered exactly what 'thisss' could be?

Miss Withers slammed her way into her office and plunged into the chair behind her desk. She didn't suggest Katie sit too.

'What do you think you were doing out there?' she repeated.

'I was . . . they were—'

'Yes. You were showing off. They were taking it all in.'

'But—'

'Don't interrupt! Out there, madam. You were glamorizing violence.'

'I wasn't, Miss.'

'Are you calling me a liar? I saw you. I heard you.'

And maybe, Katie had to admit, if she had only seen, only heard, she might indeed be forgiven for thinking that.

'I didn't mean it to sound like that.'

'Maybe not, but that's exactly how it did sound.'

'I'm sorry, Miss.'

Miss Withers' voice softened just a little. 'Well, I know you had a hard time with Ivy Toner, but I'm afraid I can't condone the methods you used to defeat her.'

Katie was puzzled. 'What do you mean, Miss?'

'The school would have handled Ivy Toner. Resorting to violence only makes you as bad as the bully.'

'But I didn't have any choice, Miss . . .'

Miss Withers was not listening. She went on, 'Violence is never the answer, Katie. And I won't have you giving younger members of the school the notion that fighting is the way to defeat bullying. That's what the staff are here for, the teachers. You come to us. We'll deal with the Ivy Toners of this world.'

'But I did come to you, Miss. And you didn't deal with it.'

Katie swallowed. Had she really just said that to Miss Withers?

The teacher's eyes narrowed. 'Ivy Toner was on her last warning.'

'She'd had her last warning three times, Miss.' Katie's voice grew strong with the unfairness of it all. 'You told me to come every time she did something, no matter how trivial. So I came. The first time, you listened. And the second. By the third time you looked at me, just the way you're looking at me now, as if I'm the troublemaker, and do you remember what you asked me, Miss?'

Miss Withers' eyes flashed, and Katie knew she did remember. But she reminded her anyway. 'You took a deep breath and you said . . . "OK, Katie, what have you done to annoy Ivy now?" '

Miss Withers' guilt lasted all of a second. 'We have always to keep an open mind, about every incident. We always have to look at both sides.'

'And that's why bullies never get beaten, and that's why people like me stop asking for help.'

She turned to leave the room.

'I haven't dismissed you yet, Katie.'

Katie didn't turn back. She wasn't going to let Miss Withers see the tears in her eyes.

'You may go, but I'll be watching you.'

She'd be watching her. Well, she wouldn't be the only one. Ivy watched her too. All day, in the playground, in the classroom. Everywhere. She was even waiting for her at the school gates.

'Don't forget, Cassidy. I'll get you . . . you and that other one.' She gave her one last sneer and ran off. Funny how that very same sneer had once terrified her, Katie thought. But not now. Not since Zan.

*

That night, snuggled once more in her bed, she tried to regain that sense of contentment and security she had felt only last night. It was all so unfair. She had stopped Ivy's bullying, and now Miss Withers was saying she was at fault.

'I'll be watching you,' she had said. Pity she hadn't watched Ivy that closely, then maybe none of this would have happened. And Ivy too, still in the shadows. And yet she wasn't so afraid of Ivy. Not now. Now she was determined to go back to enjoying her life once more. She vowed she would never get into any trouble again. She'd become a model pupil. Even Miss Withers would be proud of her.

That warm feeling was just enveloping her when she heard the phone ring downstairs.

'Katie,' her mother called. 'It's for you.'

'For me . . . at this time of night?' Reluctantly she slipped out of bed, wondering who on earth it could be. *Zan*, she decided, and she was suddenly rushing downstairs, her dressing-gown flying behind her. Zan was on the phone!

'Zan!' she shouted into the receiver. 'Is that you?'

The voice was small and timorous and nasal, and sounded as if it had been crying. 'Are you . . . Katie Cassidy?' A girl's voice, very young.

'Yes,' Katie answered. 'Who is this?'

The words tumbled out. 'You don't know me. My name's Nazeem. I'm at Notre Dame. I've got a gang always after me. The Posse, they call themselves. Always hitting me, chasing me, you know what it's like. You've got to help. I haven't got anyone else to ask.' There was another sob. 'They said they're going to get me on Friday, after school. I've got to walk past all those derelict properties on my way home. And no one will walk home with me 'cause they're dead scared of them.'

'I don't know what you think I can do.'

'You can help me, you've got to.' She was crying now, sobbing, this little girl called Nazeem. 'I've got no one else to ask. I've heard about you. Everyone has. You can turn into this Zan, and . . . help me!'

What could she say? What could she do? 'But I—'

Nazeem wouldn't let her finish. 'Promise me. Promise me you'll be there on Friday, at the school gates. Oh, promise me.'

And before she could stop herself she heard a voice saying, 'I promise.'

Katie hung up. Contentment, security, all gone. What was she going to do now?

CHAPTER FIVE

Friday morning arrived and Katie still hadn't a clue how she was going to help Nazeem. She sat at breakfast and went over all her options for the hundredth time.

'I could emigrate,' she thought. 'I could go down with some terrible illness. No one would expect me to go then.' She sighed and picked at her cornflakes.

'Or I could simply not go.' She didn't want to. She wanted to forget all about it.

Then she thought of little Nazeem, standing alone at the school gate, watching for her, and she knew she couldn't let her down. She would have to go.

If only she could find Zan. Goodness knows she'd tried. On the pretence of helping with her father's newly launched campaign for the town's homeless, she had trudged the waste ground and dumps all week looking for her. But Zan was good at hiding. Hadn't she said so?

'What is wrong with you this morning, darling?'

She glanced up at her mother. She had one leg almost wrapped around her head. Any other daughter might have giggled, but Katie was so used to her mother's eccentric behaviour she hardly blinked. 'What are you doing, Mum?'

'It's a new type of exercise programme,' she said, with a struggle. It's a difficult position to hold a conversation in. 'It's very relaxing.'

'You're sure the instruction book isn't upside-down?'

Her mother considered that. 'I think I might have done something wrong. Anyway, why are you so glum? Not more trouble at school?'

'Oh, no. Honest. I'm all right.'

'As long as you're sure . . . Ah, morning, Douglas.'

'Morning, Katherine.' Her father took his seat at the table without giving his wife a second glance. 'You coming to help me again today, Katie?'

Katie looked up. 'Today? Today's Friday.'

'Yes. And people are homeless every day of the week. You can come after school.' Her father had been delighted at her interest in his campaign, although he still hadn't quite forgiven her for Zan.

'I'll really try, Dad.' And she added quickly, 'I want to.'

'Fine,' he said, pouring himself a cup of tea. 'We're heading for the derelict properties on the west side of town this afternoon. Heard there were people sleeping rough there.'

Katie heard the words with alarm. The derelict tenements . . . Nazeem's route home! Things were getting worse by the minute.

'We just want to tell them where to come for food, soup . . . and clothes. By the way, Katherine, I looked out some of your old ones.'

Her mother shrieked. 'What old clothes!' She began trying to unravel herself.

'Trust me, dear. They're all things you don't need.' Her father carried on oblivious. 'The reporter from the local rag is going to be with us. The photographer too. Won't do any harm to get the press involved.'

Breathlessly, her mother admitted defeat. 'Will someone get me out of this!'

Katie trudged through the leaf-filled lane by the river on her way to school. November cold bit into her but she hardly felt it. Her mind was on one thing only. She couldn't think straight about that either. Suddenly the sound of a whistle, shrill and piercing, cut into the air behind her. She whirled round. There was no one to be seen, but there was someone there. She sensed it.

'Who . . .?' Her question was never finished, for just then the figure stepped into view. Red sweater, long raincoat. Zan.

'I've been looking everywhere for you.'

'I know,' Zan said. 'Your dad and his interfering bunch of do-gooders. I keep having to move on, to get away from them.'

'He's not a do-gooder!' Katie retorted so sharply, Zan's eyes widened in surprise. 'He really wants to help people. He's kind. He's—'

'OK! OK! Let's change the subject. What do you want to see me for?'

For a moment, Katie had almost forgotten all about Nazeem. It only took her a few minutes to tell Zan what had happened.

When she'd finished, Zan looked at her blankly. 'How can you be frightened of anyone daft enough to call themselves the Posse?' she snorted.

'It doesn't matter what they call themselves,' Katie protested. 'This Nazeem needs our help. We've got to help her.'

'Why?'

'Because she's being bullied. Because she has no one else to turn to. Because . . . because I promised, that's why!'

Zan shrugged. 'But why should you care? You're not being bullied any more.'

She'd been on the run, looking out for herself, just for herself, for too long, Katie decided.

'Why should you care?' Zan said again.

Katie remembered Nazeem's voice on the phone. She could almost hear it now. Frightened, tearful, alone, and she knew the answer at once. 'Because that girl was me, just a wee while ago. Terrified, and not knowing where to turn. We have to help her.'

Zan put her hands on her hips and frowned. 'We? What's this "we"? Are we a double act or something?'

Oh dear, Katie thought. Perhaps she was annoyed at the story that was going around. That she and Zan were one and the same . . .

'But you didn't want anyone to know you existed. So I thought, if everyone thinks you and me were the same—'

'Oh, I don't mind that.' She waved it away cheerfully. 'I think that's fun.'

'You helped me before, Zan. I can never thank you enough for that. But it's because of you this girl thinks I can help her. Please. I'll never ask you again.'

Zan pouted and drew a grubby hand across her face, leaving a smudged streak. Katie smiled, and Zan smiled back. 'OK, Katie. I'll do it. But I'm not doing it for this Nazeem character. I'm doing it for you.'

She tried to sound angry, but Katie was beginning to read her now. Deep down, she was every bit as soft as Katie.

'Do you think we could help her without any fighting?' At Zan's incredulous look, she hurried on. 'It's just that I'm getting a reputation . . .'

'D'you think I like fighting? No way. What's that saying, "He who fights and runs away – is a lot smarter than the one who hangs around to get beaten up".'

Katie giggled and Zan laughed too.

'I only fight when my back's against the wall. When there's no other choice. It's daft fighting otherwise.'

'So what will we do? You see, to make things worse, my dad's going to be in that area after school too. I don't know how I'm going to avoid him.'

'What area is that?' Zan asked.

'The derelict properties near Nazeem's school.'

'Aw, naw!' Zan yelled. 'That's where I've moved to. Thought I was going to be safe there for a while.' She tutted, and Katie almost apologized.

Then a strange look came on to Zan's face, and she leaned against the railings thoughtfully. 'Wait a minute . . . we could maybe make this work for us . . .'

'How? What are you thinking?'

'Maybe we shouldn't try to avoid him. I take it his usual band of merry men will be with him?'

Katie wasn't too keen on Zan's sarcastic tone, but thought it just wasn't the right time to complain. 'Yes . . .' she said.

Whatever Zan was cooking up, it was making her look very smug.

'Now remember, Katie, whatever happens, we're not seen together. I like the idea of you being me.'

'Anything you say, Zan.'

'Right then, Katie. Here's what we're going to do . . .'

Nazeem stood at the gates of Notre Dame nervously. She was very dark, and very tiny, and very frightened. She took a step back as Katie approached. She may have known her by reputation, but constant fear had made the young girl wary of any stranger.

'I'm Katie,' Katie told her at once.

Nazeem's eyes filled up with tears. 'I didn't think you were coming. I didn't know what to do. I didn't know whether to go home or stay here or . . .'

Katie began to think words tumbling out were a regular feature of Nazeem. 'I promised, didn't I?' She looked up and down the empty street. 'Where are they?'

'They'll be somewhere. They always are. They just pop out, no matter what road I take. They follow me . . .'

'OK, OK . . .'

But nothing was going to stop Nazeem in full flow. 'I take different roads, but it's always the same. And none of my friends will come with me, they're too scared . . .'

'You don't have to tell me, Nazeem, I know.'

'And there's no buses go past my way. And my father works and . . .'

'And you've complained to the teachers so often they're beginning to avoid you in the corridor.'

Nazeem nodded. 'And now I'm a big grass too. Because I told the teachers.' Her big brown eyes filled up once again. Katie felt like crying too, remembering. 'It's not fair, Katie.'

'I know, Nazeem.'

She brightened immediately, and sniffed. 'But now you're here. Everything's going to be all right.'

Oh dear, I hope so, Katie thought.

'You've got to promise me one thing, Nazeem.'

'Anything, Katie.'

'You do everything I say. Everything. Promise?'

'Oh, I promise, Katie. Goodness. You really are brave.'

If only she knew. Katie's heart was pounding in her chest. Her legs were like jelly. If she survived today, she was going to emigrate, definitely. She was going to live in seclusion. A hermit. She'd become a legend, like the yeti. Seen so little, people would never know whether she existed or not. Yes, that's exactly what she was going to do.

If she survived today, that is.

CHAPTER SIX

'And then, in history, this boy sits beside me, and he's really cheeky, copies my work. I have to hide it from him, 'cause I'm really good at history. And then in maths . . .'

Katie sighed. Nazeem had not shut up since they'd left the school gates. She'd heard about her father's job – he was a dentist. Her mother's hobby. Cooking. Her brother's course at University. Philosophy. The colour of her bedroom, pink and grey. Her hay fever, which lasted all year round, leaving her with no sense of smell. Now she had moved on to every pupil in every class she was in.

It occurred to Katie that she should have let the Posse catch Nazeem. They would let her go within five minutes, fed up listening to her.

'Then, there's this girl who sits beside me . . .'

'Ssshhh!' Katie heard something. A footstep behind her.

She turned suddenly. It was almost dark, but in the gloom, she saw a movement. Someone had darted into a close.

'They're here,' she whispered.

Nazeem froze at her side. She slipped her hand into Katie's and squeezed. 'Shouldn't we run?'

'Not yet,' Katie answered softly. 'We want them to see where we're running to.'

'I don't understand.'

'I told you, Nazeem. Don't ask questions. Just do what I tell you.'

'Can't you give me a little hint?'

A figure stepped from the shadows. Then another. Then another. Funny how they seemed to travel in threes, Katie thought. Like the Three Stooges. She had to stifle a giggle. Nerves, she thought.

The ringleader stood at the front, sneering. Trying to look tough. Managing it amazingly well. She was so like Ivy, Katie shuddered. Was there a course for bullying? she wondered. Where they learned to sneer, to look tough, to put fear into the Katies of this world? She had just got rid of Ivy, why on earth had she put herself into this position again?

Then Nazeem squeezed her hand even tighter. 'Katie . . . she . . . shouldn't we run?'

'Yes,' she answered. 'As fast as you can. Right . . . NOW!'

They were off, the Posse hard on their heels.

'No. This way!' Katie yelled as Nazeem tried to pull her round a corner.

'That way? But that way takes us right into the old properties. We'll never get out of there!'

Didn't she know it! But this was the way Zan had said to lead them. Katie trusted Zan. 'Trust me,' she said to Nazeem.

Nazeem managed a breathless smile. 'I do,' she said.

They were off again. Running as fast as they possibly could. And as she ran, Katie tried hard to remember Zan's instructions. Which corner to turn, which way to go, left or right. Oh, she hoped she was remembering it properly.

'I think we've lost them.' Nazeem said breathlessly.

'What!' Katie looked back down the empty street. 'But we can't!'

'Why?' Nazeem gasped. 'You've got a plan. haven't you? You're going to trap them? We're leading them somewhere, aren't we?'

'Yes. Yes. And yes again,' Katie answered. Suddenly there they were. Probably they knew a short cut through a back close. Goodness, she prayed, I hope they don't know too much about these old properties. Their whole plan rested on Zan's superior knowledge of living here.

'Up this close.' Katie pushed Nazeem inside, but stood at the entrance to make sure the Posse knew where she was going. They turned the corner, caught sight of her, and Katie fled after Nazeem.

'You go in there,' Katie yanked open the door of an old outside toilet. 'Hide!'

Nazeem looked shocked. 'Me! In there!'

'Yes.'

'But it's dark! . . . There's spiders . . . and goodness knows what else . . .' Her big eyes widened in alarm. 'R . . . rats.'

'There's three of them headed this way. Which do you prefer?'

That seemed to decide her. Nazeem stepped gingerly inside the room. 'I'll sneeze . . .' Katie heard her say as she shut the door on her.

'Don't you dare!' she called in to her.

Katie headed for another door at the back of the close. The right close? The right door? Oh, it must be. Now came the easy part.

'Stand by the door,' Zan had said, 'and when they come in the close, look trapped, look scared.'

72

Well, that wouldn't be hard. Right this minute, Katie was terrified. Her hand shook as she held the rusty knob of the door. Suddenly, they were there at the mouth of the close, silhouetted against the fading light. Katie couldn't make out their faces, but she could imagine their triumphant grins.

'Where's wee Nazeem?' the leader of them asked.

Katie pressed herself against the door as if she was barring their way. 'You're not getting her.'

This struck them as funny. When the leader laughed, her two dumb lieutenants laughed too.

'She's in there? You think you're protecting her or somethin'?' She turned to the other two. 'See that? That's the great Katie Cassidy we've been hearin' aboot. See how clever she is. Runnin' here, of a' places. Oh, dead smart.' This sent them into gales of laughter.

Katie slowly began to turn the knob of the door.

'She's got wee Nazeem in there, and we're goin' to get her. In fact . . . we're goin' to get the two o' you.'

She lunged. Katie swung open the door and jumped. One great leap. Zan had told her, and she would avoid the hole in the floor. The one the homeless who had slept here had warned each other about. The one Zan knew about, and the Posse didn't. Katie landed on solid floor. The Posse didn't. They threw themselves inside and disappeared, landing in an untidy heap on the rubble below. 'They won't get hurt,' Zan had promised. 'It's only a couple of feet. But they will be confused, and that's how we want them. They won't know what's happening.' And they didn't.

'Mary, where are we?'

'Somethin' touched me there.'

'Hey, where is she?'

'I'm here,' Katie said, and although the room was almost pitch black, there was enough light to see their frightened, apprehensive faces. Little Nazeem's had looked just like that when Katie had first seen her.

'What are you goin' to do to us?' one of them asked, trying to sound defiant.

'Me? Nothing,' Katie answered truthfully. She stepped back, and a moment later it was Zan's face they saw, just dimly.

'But I am,' she said, and she pushed the door closed and pitch blackness slammed into the room.

'Over here, Mr Cassidy. I'm sure I hear something.'

Katie's father and some of his campaign helpers stood at the edge of the close. The cries were faint but they could still hear them.

'Yes. There's someone in there,' Katie's father said. They began running into the close. 'Probably one of the old drunks, living in here. Could be suffering from hypothermia.'

'Hypothermia?' At the sound of the word the man with the camera began pushing his way forward. 'Come on, Eddie.' He shouted to the reporter behind him. 'We might get a good picture out of this.'

When Katie's father flung open the door, the photographer was right behind him. 'There's something down there . . .' He swung the torch into the basement and a gasp went up from the group gathered round him. The photographer's camera flashed with excitement.

He had managed to get his good picture at last.

It was front page news in the local paper next day. Not a story about the tramps or the homeless, but a picture of the Posse, tied up, sitting back to back in the basement, looking slightly ridiculous, with a placard placed around their necks: 'THIS IS WHAT HAPPENS TO BULLIES'.

Her father looked up from his paper. 'Did you have anything to do with this, Katie?' She blushed and looked away. 'They said you did,' he continued. 'They said, "Katie Cassidy did this." Did you?'

'No.' And this time she wasn't lying, so she could say it boldly.

'These girls could have you charged, you know.'

'Have you spoken to Nazeem Parikh, Dad? Those three have been making her life a misery for months. She asked me to help her. All I did was walk home with her. Those three chased us all the way. They chased us into those derelict buildings and fell into a hole. How can I be to blame for that?'

'Who tied them up? Who put that placard round their necks?'

'Maybe someone who wanted to help Nazeem too. And what did they do to them anyway, Dad? They tied them up to stop them following us. They put a placard round their necks to say they were bullies and they are!'

'It made them look foolish.'

'Good!' Katie knew she was angry and couldn't help it. 'Maybe now they won't bully anyone else. If that story and that picture means they won't make anyone else afraid – good!' she repeated. 'What do you think they would have done to Nazeem and me if they'd caught us? Have you thought about that?' She felt the tears spring to her eyes. 'Why should I have to say all this, Dad? Why weren't you so concerned when it was happening to me? You told me to stand up for myself. Now I have. Remember, Ivy Toner almost pushed me off a wall. She could have killed me. They shoved my head down a toilet. How foolish do you think I looked then?'

Her dad wasn't saying a word. His face was ashen, his mouth hanging open.

'It didn't seem to worry you so much when it was just me, did it? But we can't have the bad guys looking foolish, can we? We can't turn the tables on them. They weren't hurt. We made sure of that. I don't think they would have been so thoughtful to us. Do you?' She stood up, the tears streaming from her eyes. Her mother came running down the stairs wrapped in a pink towel.

'Douglas . . . Katie . . . what on earth's going on?'

'Why didn't you start a campaign to help me!' The thought had been eating into her for a long time. 'There's probably more children being bullied in this town than there are homeless anyway!'

She ran from the house to the school, and when she went in through the school gates her eyes were red-rimmed from crying. There was an admiring crowd waiting for her.

'I don't know why you're looking so sad,' one of them said. 'You're a heroine. Everybody's talking about you.'

That didn't make her feel good at all. Miss Withers would have something to say about that. Ivy Toner too. Even more reason to go after Zan. She had to protect Zan from that. She understood that now, more than ever. Problems seemed to be piling up for Katie.

There were even more at three thirty as she came out of the school gates. Nazeem was waiting for her.

She beamed a smile. 'Katie!' She grabbed at her hand and held it. 'I'm so proud that you are my very best friend.'

'I am?'

'Of course. And now, everyone wants to talk to me, because I know you . . . and Zan, of course.'

'Zan?'

'I know. She doesn't really exist. She's you. You're magic, Katie.' Nazeem sighed. 'I've never known anyone magic before.'

'I'm not magic, Nazeem.'

'You are to me,' Nazeem said. And nothing would convince her otherwise.

'Anyway, what are you doing here?'

'I'm going home with you. My mother and my father

are coming to your house when my father finishes surgery. By the way, if you ever need anything doing to your teeth he'll do it for nothing. He hasn't actually said that yet, but I'm going to speak to him about it.'

'They're coming to my house?' Katie managed to squeeze in.

'To thank you, Katie. You're the only one who helped me. And I don't think the Posse will bother anyone in our school again. Everyone's been laughing and laughing at them. That photo was stuck up everywhere.'

For a moment that made her feel good. She was glad for Nazeem's sake, and for all the others. But to have Nazeem as a lifelong friend? Was this the price she had to pay? If she would just stop talking for five minutes. But it was hopeless. By the time they reached home, Katie knew every stick of furniture in Nazeem's house, the whole family's birthdays and every meal they'd eaten in the past three months.

Yet it was good Nazeem was there when they did get home. Her mother was delighted to meet her, and took to Nazeem at once. Probably she saw in her a kindred spirit. And it broke the ice between her father and herself. Nazeem's animated chatter exhausted and relaxed everyone at the same time. Yet Katie knew what had been said that morning would hang between them for a long time.

The phone rang just as her mother had organized them all in the living-room for some tea. It was her mother who answered it.

'It's for you, Katie. A girl.'

She had a deep sense of foreboding as she lifted the receiver. Not another girl in trouble. She couldn't handle all that again.

But this time, it was Zan.

'You didn't tell me your dad had the press with him.'

Katie was puzzled. 'I'm sorry. I forgot. Does it matter? I thought that the picture . . .'

Zan didn't let her finish. 'I told you. I didn't want any publicity. I was mentioned in that article.'

'Only as the homeless girl on the dump who inspired my dad's campaign.'

'That just might be enough.'

'It's only the local paper, Zan. No one outside the town ever reads it.'

She heard her sigh. 'I hope so, Katie. I really hope so.'

Katie stood by the phone for a long time before she rejoined the others. What could Zan's secret be? What was it that made her, who was afraid of nothing, so afraid?

CHAPTER SEVEN

'I think Nazeem is absolutely sweet,' Katie's mother said. They had just waved the family off that night.

'You think everyone's absolutely sweet, Katherine,' her father said. There was so much tenderness in the way he said it. So much love in the smile her mother flashed back at him.

'She never seems to take a breath. She talks non-stop.' Katie had spent most of the evening in her bedroom with Nazeem, and she was exhausted.

'Doesn't she,' her mother agreed, as if it was another of her absolutely sweet bits. 'She just chatters on like a little bird.'

Her father yawned. 'I don't know about anyone else, but I'm exhausted.'

'Me too.' Katie didn't quite meet her father's eyes, though she knew he was looking at her. She wasn't ready to smile at him, not yet.

'Right, I'll make us all a nightcap, shall I?'

Katie and her father groaned at the same time. One of her mother's nightcaps was usually some herbal concoction guaranteed to put hairs on your chest.

They were sitting round the fire gingerly sipping their 'nightcap', when the doorbell rang.

'At this time of night?' Katie's mother jumped up and peeked through the curtains of the bay window. Katie and her father took the opportunity to deposit the remains of the 'nightcap' in adjacent plant pots. Usually this operation was accompanied by winks and giggles. This time they did it quite stiffly, not looking at each other.

'Oh my heavens, it's two policemen!'

Her father didn't waste a minute hurrying to the door, and moments later he was leading the two officers into the living-room.

'It's actually you they want to see, Katie.' Her father's voice was stern.

Katie sat bolt upright. 'Me!'

'I'm afraid we've had a complaint, young lady,' the first policeman said. She noticed he had ginger hair growing out of his nose.

'Those three girls who were assaulted last night—' the second began, but Katie interrupted him.

'Assaulted! They chased us all the way home from school.'

'Nevertheless they were tied up against their will. That is assault.'

Katie shook her head. 'I don't believe this.'

'Neither do I,' said her mother. 'What exactly are you here for?'

'We had the parents of those girls at the station today. They wanted to charge your daughter.'

'With what?' her father asked.

'These girls say your daughter was the one who assaulted them and tied them up.'

But it wasn't me . . .! The words almost tumbled from her. She held her breath. She couldn't deny it. She had to protect Zan.

The younger policeman had the bluest eyes she had ever seen. Now they looked embarrassed. 'These girls don't actually say it was you . . . They had some nonsensical story about how you turned into someone else, but their parents believe it had to be you.'

'That's the only reason you're not being charged. Because they do stick to that ridiculous story.'

'Charged with what, Constable?' Katie could almost see the anger rising in her mother. 'My daughter and her friend were chased by these girls, intent on doing them harm. And you are telling me . . . my Katie . . . could be charged!'

Blue-eyes looked embarrassed again. 'The point is, Mrs Cassidy . . .' he could obviously see her mother was ready to explode '. . . we know these girls. We've had trouble with them before. But our hands are tied. If they make a complaint, we have to follow it up.'

The other policeman, Ginger, smiled at Katie. 'Just stay away from them, Katie. Well away.'

Exactly what she had been told when she had complained in school about Ivy. 'Stay away from her, Katie.' 'Go a different road home from school, Katie.' 'Avoid her, Katie.' 'Don't give her any trouble, Katie.'

'And what about little Nazeem? They're in her school. They've been making her life miserable for months.'

'I dare say, Katie,' her mother said archly, 'little Nazeem's also been told not to annoy them any more.'

Ginger's smile disappeared. 'We're only doing our job, Mrs Cassidy. If Katie or this other little girl have any more trouble, they can let us know immediately. We'll deal with it.'

Her mother slipped an arm around Katie's shoulders and pulled her close. 'You don't have to worry about Katie going anywhere near the likes of them. But I think it's absolutely shameful that after everything she's been through, it's my daughter who gets a warning from the police.'

So did Katie. As her parents saw the policemen out she couldn't stop thinking about the unfairness of it all.

'It makes me so angry!' her mother said as she came back into the room.

Her father stood at the door. He had been quieter than Katie had expected all the time the police were in the house.

Finally, he spoke. 'OK, Katie. What's going on? I want to know the truth.'

'Leave her be, Douglas.'

'The truth about what, Dad?'

'Who is this other girl who keeps popping up when you're around?'

Katie's mouth went dry. 'What other girl?'

'The other girl all these fools seem to think is you. And don't say she doesn't exist, or she is you. Because I don't believe either of those.' He waited a moment for an answer, but for the life of her Katie couldn't think of a thing to say.

'Is she the girl in the cardboard box? The one you first told us about?' Again he only waited for a moment for an answer. 'Tell me, Katie. I only want to help her.'

And Katie knew he did. She knew that if she admitted Zan's existence, he would do everything in his power to find her, to track her down. To help her, to put her back where she didn't want to go. And Katie knew too that she could never allow that. Even if it meant lying to her father. 'I . . . told you before. There is no other girl. I made her up.'

Her father's face froze. Even her mother's gentle expression hardened a little. 'We know that isn't true,' her father said. 'Why are you lying?'

The best form of defence is attack. Katie had read that somewhere. She decided to test the truth of it right now. 'You always said I was to stand up for myself. Face up to my problems. Well, I did. And now it seems I'm the bad one. I've just had the police here ready to charge me, for helping wee Nazeem! And do you care? Any of you? What kind of parents are you?' And she fled from the room in tears.

Later, as she lay in bed unable to sleep, she counted the growing pile of problems she had, instead of sheep. Miss Withers was one. Distrustful, blaming her for something, watching her. Then there was Ivy Toner. She knew she was going to have to be careful where Ivy was concerned. Now she'd had a warning from the police (she could still hardly believe that) to keep away from the Posse. She wondered for a moment whether having acquired Nazeem as a lifelong friend should be considered as one of her problems, but she discounted it. That was cruel.

And the most important problem of all. Her parents didn't trust her. And could she blame them? They knew she was lying to them, and she so desperately wanted to tell them the truth. If only she could understand why it was so important to Zan to remain invisible, not to exist at all. All she did know was that she, Katie, was all Zan had in the world, the only friend. Just as Zan, only a few weeks ago, had been the only friend Katie had had.

She would never betray her. Never!

'What's all this?' Zan eyed suspiciously the case Katie had brought with her. They were together in one of the derelict properties not far from where the Posse had met their come-uppance.

Katie opened the case. 'Shirt,' she said, and threw Zan a green shirt. 'Jeans.' The jeans landed on Zan's head.

'Shoes.' She turned a quizzical eye on Zan's feet. 'What size do you take?'

'Size?' Zan looked baffled.

Katie shrugged. 'I don't suppose it matters. You'll fit into them anyway. And here's a nice warm sweater and an anorak.'

'What's all this for? Am I going somewhere?'

'And two packs of new knickers.' Zan caught those deftly.

'You think I need a change of clothes or something?'

'I think you stink,' Katie said, and both of them fell into a fit of giggles.

It was Sunday afternoon. Katie's mother and father had gone for a drive. Her excuse for not going with them, extra homework. More lies.

'My dad said I should be giving clothes to the homeless. And you are homeless, aren't you? Go on, put them on.'

Katie watched in amazement as Zan changed. She had never seen anything like it. One half of a shirt off, the new one on. The other half off and she slipped her arm into the sleeve of the new green shirt. Same with the trousers. One leg of the new pair was slipped into before she took her other leg out of the old ones.

Zan laughed as Katie watched. 'It's a knack you get

when you have to change in the freezing cold.' She started to pull on the sweater. 'So I have your father to thank for all this.' She said it with a sneer. Katie wished she could make her like him, love him even, as she did. 'Is he talking to you yet?' Zan went on.

'You can't blame him for being hurt. He knows I'm lying to him. And I've never lied to him before.'

Zan pulled the sweater over her head quickly so she could see Katie's face. 'You'll tell him about me, and I'll never forgive you. I'll leave here so fast . . . and I'll never come back.'

'I won't,' Katie reassured her. 'I promise. It's not just that, anyway,' she sighed. 'It's this police thing. We've never been involved with the police before. I still can't get over them coming to give me a warning.'

'Nothing would surprise me about the police. Did you expect them to believe you? To help you? Ha! I bet you still believe in Santa Claus!'

There was a bitterness in her voice that Katie just couldn't understand. 'What did the police do to you, Zan?' she asked softly. But she knew she wouldn't answer. She never answered any of Katie's questions about her past. 'Don't ever ask,' was all she would say.

'Ta-Ra! There, how do I look?'

Katie gasped as Zan began to strut about like a model on a catwalk, wearing Katie's sweater and Katie's shirt, with Katie's anorak draped across one shoulder.

'Well, what do you think?'

What did she think? It was like looking into a mirror.

'Why, Zan,' she said at last. 'You look exactly like me.'

Her parents were at home. She saw their car as she turned into her street. Katie had her excuses for being out all ready. She had simply felt like a walk. It was a brisk November day and her parents, who loved walking and encouraged it, would understand that.

It was only as she drew nearer to her own house that she noticed another car parked behind her parents'. A dark green Volvo, battered and old, like a tank. Menacing. The very look of it made Katie shiver.

She hurried up the path to her house and opened the door.

'Katie, is that you?' her mother called.

'I went for a walk, Mum.'

'That's OK, dear. Come in here. There's someone wants to meet you.'

There was a stranger sitting on the sofa beside her mother, a thin man in a dark green raincoat. He stood up as Katie came into the living-room and she was astounded at his length. His face was long and thin too, and his dark eyes were sunk deep into the sockets. She knew the old Volvo was his. It so resembled him. Menacing.

He tried a smile, but only his mouth made it. His eyes stayed sombre, watching her closely.

'This is Mr Whittaker, Katie,' her mother said.

'Hello.' She sounded more nervous than she meant to.

'Hello, Katie.' His voice was very soft, and very low.

It was her father who spoke next, watching closely for her reaction to his words. 'Mr Whittaker's a private detective, Katie. He's come all the way from London.' He paused, and Katie held her breath. 'He's looking for the girl in the cardboard box.'

CHAPTER EIGHT

'But I tell you there is no girl. I made her up.'

Katie had been trying to convince her parents and this Mr Whittaker for the last half-hour. She had a feeling they still didn't believe her.

'I don't mean her any harm, Katie.' Mr Whittaker's words flowed from his mouth like smooth chocolate. 'You must believe that.'

Katie didn't. Something about his unsmiling eyes, the low voice, something she didn't trust.

'Why don't you tell us the reason you want to find her then?'

'I'm a private investigator, Katie.'

How she wished he wouldn't use her name in every sentence. She didn't trust that either.

'There is such a thing as client confidentiality.' His eyes narrowed. She had a feeling he was trying to smile again. 'You understand what client confidentiality means, don't you, Katie?'

As if she didn't know what it meant indeed! Well, she didn't! But she'd look it up later. For the moment she concentrated on looking intelligent.

'Mr Whittaker has to have his client's permission before he can tell you who they are, or why they want to find this girl,' her father explained.

'Can I just say this, Mr Cassidy? And I don't think I'm breaking the trust of my clients at all when I say it, but,' he looked again at Katie, directing his words only at her, 'there are thousands of children disappear each year. Some of them are never found. Their parents are left not knowing what happened to them. Some of these parents spend the rest of their lives searching for their children.' He paused, a little too much like an actor playing a part for Katie's liking. 'Some of them hire people like me, Katie.'

There he went with the 'Katie' again.

'I know I would,' her mother said, drawing Katie to her as if she might disappear at any moment. 'I'd never give up trying to find my child.'

'I have a news-clipping service,' Mr Whittaker went on, 'sends me any stories about girls, just about this age, begging in the streets, homeless, whatever. Then I follow it up. I have followed so many false trails over the past few months, you wouldn't believe.'

'Well, that's what this is, a false trail,' Katie burst out. 'There is no homeless girl living on the dump. I made her up.' She swallowed. 'I lied.'

Mr Whittaker's deep sunk eyes never left her. 'But . . . she keeps cropping up in other stories.'

Katie shrugged. She didn't know what to say to that. She couldn't try to tell him she was the other girl. Not in front of her parents.

'Katie!' Her father's voice was stern. 'No one means this girl any harm. It's nonsense carrying on with this story that she doesn't exist!'

'I don't know why you won't believe me. Why would I lie about it?' She forced herself to look at Mr Whittaker, though something in those eyes made her shiver. 'I'm sorry, but you may as well go. You're wasting your time.' And she fled from the living-room and up the stairs before anyone could say another word.

'Leave her be, Katherine,' she heard her father say. 'She's not going to change her story.'

Katie listened, her bedroom door ajar.

'Why would she lie, Douglas? She's never lied to us before.'

'I'm sorry, Mr Whittaker,' her father said. 'And perhaps my wife's right. Perhaps Katie is telling the truth. I've been all over this town, the derelict properties, the dump, and I've seen no sign of this girl either.'

Katie held her breath, waiting for Whittaker's reply. 'Please,' she prayed, 'let him go away. Let him forget all about Zan.'

Finally, Mr Whittaker answered. 'If you don't mind, Mr Cassidy, I'll just hang about the town for a bit. I know it might be for nothing. But my clients wouldn't want me to give up without making sure.'

That night Katie had yet another worry to add to all the rest. Mr Whittaker! Maybe Zan wasn't the girl he was looking for. She couldn't be. Katie imagined his clients, loving, caring parents – just like her own. No, he couldn't be looking for Zan. She wouldn't be afraid to go back if she had parents like that.

Yet . . . if it wasn't Zan he was looking for, why was Katie so afraid he might find her?

She was still thinking it over as she trailed her schoolbag into class next day. So lost in thought she didn't hear the door slam behind her, or realize that she was alone in the classroom with her arch enemy. Ivy!

'Think you're pretty smart, don't ye?'

Katie jumped out of her reverie at the sound of the voice. 'What?'

'Don't act the wee miss innocent wi' me, Cassidy. You might have scared the Posse oot of their knickers, but no' me. No' Ivy Toner.'

No' much, Katie wanted to say. She certainly hadn't given Katie any trouble since Zan had scared the knickers off Ivy. The thought of it made Katie giggle. This was the last thing Ivy could stand. Her eyes bulged, her face went red. She would have lunged at Katie. Katie was even ready to make a quick getaway if she did. But just at that moment the classroom erupted with noise. The door was flung open and a group of pupils came in, surrounding the teacher. Saved in the nick of time. Ivy glared at her, and mouthed, 'I'll get you, Cassidy. That's a promise.'

Ivy was going to find it hard to keep that promise, for Katie was never alone now. She was always surrounded by friends, or adoring fans, as Miss Withers sneeringly called them. It would be difficult to pick on anyone when they were always in a crowd. Wasn't that what Zan had said? Stick together. It was the ones who were always on their own who were at risk. The ones who were different.

It was break time and Katie and her friends stood at the bike sheds, laughing and talking. Through the crowds Katie glimpsed Ivy, heading in her direction, and she steeled herself for a confrontation.

Without Zan?

She was almost relieved when she realized it wasn't her Ivy was headed for. It was Teresa Henderson. Teresa Henderson was always alone. No one ever bothered with her. She was dirty. She had really bad breath. There was always an unwashed smell about her, and when you touched her hand (which no one ever did willingly) it was always cold and clammy. She was standing alone in the playground. She had both hands shoved in her mouth, managing to chew ten nails at once. It was probably the only time they got washed, Katie thought, and she was angry at herself for thinking that. She was as bad as the rest. She avoided Teresa Henderson, just like everyone else. Including Ivy.

So . . . why was Ivy heading for her now?

Teresa looked up as Ivy stopped in front of her, and blinked nervously several times. Ivy began to talk to her, prodding her with her finger so that Teresa stumbled back. And as Teresa listened, she cowered. Katie knew a cower when she saw one. She had cowered herself often enough when Ivy threatened her. Of course, she'd had no trouble from Ivy. But that didn't mean to say no one else had. Bullies move on to fresh pastures. It was Teresa's turn now. Teresa. She wouldn't ask a teacher for help. People like Teresa expect to get bullied. People like Teresa wouldn't ask anyone for help. Unlike amiable, happy little Nazeem, Teresa wouldn't believe anyone would want to help her. And wasn't it true? Not one soul in that playground, except Katie, was even glancing in her direction. Ivy could bully and threaten her as much as she wanted. It was only Teresa Henderson, after all.

'Look over there,' Katie said. One of the girls around her turned to see. Teresa was passing over some money now, hurriedly.

The girl laughed. 'Ivy's taking a chance. She might catch something!'

They all laughed at that. All except Katie. 'You sound as if you're on Ivy's side.'

'Oh, come on, Katie. It's only dirty Teresa Henderson.'

Katie looked round them all. The look on her face

made them stop laughing. 'It was only me a few weeks ago.'

She looked over again to where Ivy and Teresa stood. Teresa was trying to laugh now, trying to please Ivy with a smile, just as Katie used to do. She suddenly knew she had to do something.

This time she was alone. No Zan. Here, in the playground, no hope of Zan coming to the rescue. She still had to do something.

She wasn't alone, she reminded herself. Her friends were here. She looked round them and wondered how long they would remain her friends if Ivy beat her now.

'Are you coming?' she asked them.

'Over there?'

'To help wee dirty Teresa?'

'Are you coming, or aren't you?' Katie repeated. 'If we stick together, no one can get us. Can't you see that?'

They weren't going to come. It was written all over their faces. They were afraid, scared still of the Ivys of this world. She was going to have to go over there herself. A little part of her began to panic. Now she'd said it, she'd have to. Why couldn't she ever keep her mouth shut? She tried one last time.

'If we all go over there together, Ivy's not going to

bother anyone again. If she sees we're going to help all the dirty wee Teresas in the school, who's left for her to pick on?'

There was silence. Then, one by one, the look on each of their faces began to change. Katie could read this new look easily. It said simply, 'If there is any trouble, she can turn into Zan!'

They were expecting more magic.

'Katie's right,' someone said, boldly now. 'Let's stick with Katie.'

Ivy looked up as they approached. 'Whit do you lot want?' she asked gruffly.

'You leave Teresa alone,' Katie said.

Ivy's jaw hung open, not believing what she'd just heard. 'Whit did you say?'

'Has she taken any money off you, Teresa?'

Teresa flushed and swallowed. She looked from Katie and the girls around her, to Ivy. None of these girls were her friends. Could she trust any of them? Katie read that in her grimy face.

'Come over here,' Katie said gently. She reached out and took Teresa's hand. It was cold and clammy and made her cringe, but she held it tight and drew her gently into her circle of friends. One of us.

'Did she take money from you?' Katie had to look up to Teresa, who was tall, though seldom looked it. She smiled and said gently again, 'Did she?'

At last Teresa nodded.

Katie looked at Ivy. 'Give it back, then.'

Ivy glared around them, trying to look fierce. It had always worked so well, that look. But she was alone now.

'Aye, give it back,' a voice behind Katie shouted.

'Or else,' another voice threatened.

Katie almost giggled then. She had a feeling she knew what the 'or else' might be. She, Katie, would turn into Zan. Whatever it was, it worked.

Anger exploded in Ivy. But an anger tinged with fear. 'Here, take your money back!' She threw a handful of coins at them. 'It's the last time I ask you for a loan for anythin', Teresa Henderson.'

She stalked away, not looking back once. But she heard. Heard the laughter and the cheers that erupted as she left them. And Ivy would never forget that, Katie knew. Nor would she forgive.

She told Zan about it later when they met after school.

'Didn't I tell you? Stick together. They can't touch

you if you all stick together.' Zan smiled and popped another crisp into her mouth. She looks amazingly like me, Katie thought, watching her.

'You should get your hair cut,' Katie said.

'I do cut it.' She held out an uneven chunk for Katie's inspection. 'Do it myself.'

'I don't mean that, I mean properly. In a hairdresser's.'

Zan stopped chewing. 'Don't try to make me what I'm not. I'm happy the way I am. OK?'

'OK,' Katie said, though she still couldn't understand.

'So now you have another fan. This Teresa?'

'Oh, I hope not. Nazeem's bad enough.'

'I've never heard anyone talk so much,' Zan laughed. She had a hearty laugh that echoed in the old empty tenement.

'Anyway,' Katie reminded her, 'they're really your fans. Zan is the one they think helped them.'

'Not today, Katie. Today, it was you. Only you.'

That hadn't occurred to Katie before. She had stood up to Ivy. She, little Katie Cassidy. The thought made her feel warm all over.

'I'm so glad I met you, Zan.'

'You've paid me back,' Zan answered. 'Because of you, I can stay here. Everyone thinks I'm you. You're me. I don't exist. I feel safe for once. I've never stayed this long anywhere before.'

As she spoke Katie remembered Mr Whittaker, with his long dark face, and his questions . . . and the warm feeling went.

Zan saw the change in Katie's expression. 'What is it? What's wrong?'

Katie almost didn't tell her. It would be stupid to worry her for nothing. But she knew she couldn't lie. Not to Zan. And she would have to warn her. Mr Whittaker was planning to join in her father's frequent forays to search out vagrants.

'It's probably nothing,' Katie said. 'He can't be looking for you.'

Zan sat up rigid. 'Who?'

'Mr Whittaker. He's a private investigator. It can't be you he's looking for. His clients are parents, their child disappeared. They're frantic with worry. It can't be you.' She had to make her stay. She had to.

'But he's not leaving?'

'In a few days. I told him you don't exist. I think he believed me.'

'You THINK he believed you!' Zan was suddenly shouting at her. 'Don't you realize yet how important this is to me?'

Katie hurried on. 'But I told him it isn't you. It can't be.' She paused, all at once afraid. 'Is it?'

Zan closed her eyes almost as if she were praying. The deserted close was silent, the traffic noises from the streets faded and distant . . .

'You know what?' she said at last. And even then Katie knew what was coming. Zan drew in a deep breath. 'I can't stay here, Katie. I have to leave right away.'

CHAPTER NINE

Nothing Katie said could convince Zan that it was safe for her to stay. Only the fact that this Mr Whittaker would be leaving soon himself had made her promise to hang on for a few more days.

If only Katie could do something to convince him Zan didn't exist. If only she could come up with a plan; but her mind was completely blank of brilliant ideas. She could think of nothing except . . . Zan had to stay. If she left, why . . . it would be like losing part of herself.

'What's wrong, dear? You look so worried.' Her mother brought her a cup of tea and sat down on the bed beside her. 'You're supposed to be doing your homework.' Her homework lay untouched on her desk in the corner. 'If it's the police you're worried about, they won't bother you again.'

Katie had forgotten all about the police. Their visit had been drowned in a sea of more troubles.

'As long as you don't go near those three girls again. And of course you won't,' her mother tutted. 'I know it's unfair. And I've written to the Chief Constable about it. I'm very angry.'

Katie smiled for the first time that night. Her mother, trying to be so serious, was wearing a bright pink tracksuit and a face mask, and she had two halves of a lemon tied on to her head. It was difficult to keep a straight face. 'I'm letting the juice seep through to give my hair shine,' she had explained earlier to Katie's father. He had almost jumped out of his skin when she first came out of the bathroom. 'Alien Invasion! Alien Invasion!' he had shouted, leaping over the banister and firing an imaginary space gun at her. Katie smiled again at the memory of the moment. So much like old times. Katie would normally have joined in. She knew her father had been hoping she would too. She just couldn't; not tonight.

'There! My wee girl's smiling again.' Mum couldn't smile back, not without cracking the face mask. So she just hugged her. 'Now, drink up your tea.'

Katie was trying to avoid that. If her mother left the room she could surely find one plant left alive to deposit the dreaded brew. But tonight, her mother was determined to watch Katie sample her latest concoction.

'Come on,' she urged. 'Drink up. It's good for you.'

Katie took a sip and wished she hadn't. There was garlic in this one, and something that tasted vaguely of crushed dandelions – ones that had been kept well watered by the town's cats.

'That will send you to sleep,' her mother assured her.

'For ever,' Katie added silently.

'And I want you to wake up tomorrow and start enjoying life. Like you used to.'

Katie knew she should try, but Zan just wouldn't stay out of her mind for long. She thought about her in history, and got herself into trouble. She worried about her in maths, and got into more trouble. She was still thinking about her in PE when Mr Percy's voice boomed out and almost sent her spinning off the bench in the gym.

'Katie Cassidy! You haven't heard a thing I've been saying, have you?'

'Yes, I have sir,' she lied.

'OK. Repeat.'

She looked round for help, trying to lip-read the mouthed instructions the rest of the class were giving her. It was no use.

'Not a clue,' Mr Percy admitted for her. 'Well, since you're obviously not interested in what I've been saying, perhaps you'd like to do something else instead . . .?'

'Me?' Her very worst subject was PE. She hated sports. The only thing she even remotely liked was badminton, and she wasn't good at that.

'Yes, you. Three laps round the gym. Running. Full speed. Right now!'

There was no arguing with Mr Percy. When he said go, you went. She was only half-way round when she'd had enough. But she knew from experience that she could fall down and die in the gym, and he would not take pity on her. He wasn't called No Mercy Percy for nothing.

She passed him, breathing hard. Any sensible man would have had her on oxygen. Mr Percy ignored her. He kept on talking to the rest of the class.

'A wonderful gym . . . and I think we should be making more use of its facilities . . .'

Like life-saving classes, Katie might have suggested, if she'd had the breath.

Second time around she stopped, panting, beside him. The rest of the class were already giggling, as they usually did when Katie did sports. She bent and rested her hands on her knees.

'Did . . . you say . . . two . . . laps . . . sir . . .?' she suggested hopefully.

'Three!' he snapped. 'Now run!'

And Katie was off again, her legs almost buckling under her.

'So . . . have we any suggestions for a class after school? And let's learn something useful at the same time.'

'Ballroom dancing?' There was a collective groan, and the suggester of that one almost went flying off the bench too.

'Sword fencing?'

'In this school!' Mr Percy boomed again. 'You lot would have wiped out each other within the week.'

'Sir . . . sir . . .' Katie struggled to get the words out.

He turned. 'Did you say something, Cassidy?'

'Sel . . . l . . . l . . .'

'Out with it, girl.'

Couldn't he see she was trying? She might die first.

'Self-defence classes, sir.'

Then she fell in a heap on the floor. If he wanted her to finish this final lap, he'd have to carry her round himself.

Mr Percy stroked his chin thoughtfully. 'Mmm, interesting idea. Any particular reason why you suggested that one, Cassidy?'

'I think if we learned to defend ourselves –' she took another deep breath '– we'd be able to take care of ourselves more . . .'

'Defend yourself? Against what?'

'There are such things as bullies, sir.'

There was a murmur of approval and agreement. Mr Percy glanced at them. 'The rest of you agree?'

'It's a great idea, sir.'

'Aye. Self-defence. Brilliant.'

'Can you teach us that, sir?'

'But who's to say the bullies won't take up the self-defence classes too?' was Mr Percy's next question.

'Because that's not how they fight,' Katie answered at once. 'But if they come, well, let them. At least they won't be able to pick on us if we can take care of ourselves.'

'That's actually a rather sensible suggestion, Cassidy.' He sounded slightly astonished, as if a sensible suggestion was the last thing he would have expected from her.

The rest of the class once again murmured their approval.

'Let me see what I can organize,' Mr Percy told them as he dismissed them from class.

Katie sat in her bedroom, trying to concentrate on her history project. All she could think of was Zan.

'Is Mr Whittaker still here?' She had asked her father at teatime. They were still not on the best of terms. Something hung between them. That something was

Zan, and the lies she was telling to protect her.

'He's still here,' he had answered.

'He must be leaving soon, though. If he's not able to find this . . . mysterious girl . . . what's the point of him staying?'

'He won't give up so easily, Katie.' He was trying to make her understand. 'His clients . . . this girl's parents . . . are desperate to find their child. I can understand that. The man has to make sure. I think he's going to interview . . .' he hesitated '. . . these girls you had trouble with.'

'But Ivy Toner'll say there is another girl . . . because she would lose face if wee Katie Cassidy beat her.'

'He wants to talk to them anyway.'

'And of course he'll believe her before he believes me!' And then she added, just because she wanted to hurt him. 'Just like you do.'

It was another worry to add to the others. Of course, the Posse would insist Katie and Zan were one and the same. So would Lindy and Michelle. But Ivy . . . Ivy was another matter altogether.

Oh, she had to think of something to help Zan, to keep her safe, here with Katie.

'Look who's come to see you, darling.' Her mother blocked the doorway and stepped aside to reveal Nazeem.

'Katie! I haven't seen you for days!' Nazeem's bright smile lit up the room. So much for Katie's history project, and thinking up a plan to save Zan.

Her mother left them, and Nazeem immediately threw herself on the bed. That was Nazeem. Everything she did, she threw herself into. She began to chatter about her family, the postman's bad feet and the letter he had brought from her aunt in India. The good thing about Nazeem was you didn't have to listen to her. The bad thing was you couldn't concentrate on anything else. And here she was trying desperately to work out a plan.

'And I told him. You're just magic. I can't say anything more, I told him. Katie's just magic.'

'I'm what . . .?' Katie was pulled back to Nazeem's conversation. 'What are you talking about?'

'Aren't you listening?'

Katie tried to look as if she had been.

'That Mr Whittaker came. I don't like him, Katie. He gives me the creeps. He was asking all sorts of questions.'

Katie sat upright. 'And what did you tell him?'

'So silly. He was trying to get me to say there was

another girl that day. She was the one that tied up the Posse.' She tutted and rolled her big eyes, as if anyone could be that stupid. 'But I just told him. There was no other girl. It was you. You came and saved me.'

'Good, Nazeem.'

'I wasn't going to let any other girl get the credit. So I just told him. Katie's magic. She can turn into this other girl whenever she wants.'

Katie's feelings went from relief to apprehension. He was either going to think everyone in this town was a half-wit or (and this was what frightened her) he was still going to follow the trail that might lead him to Zan.

'I did right, didn't I, Katie? I know you said you're not magic, but . . .' Nazeem smiled. Nothing would ever convince her otherwise. 'I know the truth.' She went prattling on. 'Although actually I don't know why I should be so loyal to someone who totally ignores me.'

'Me?' Katie said. 'When have I ever ignored you? When would I ever get the chance?'

Nazeem tutted. 'Yesterday, it was. As I was going home from school.'

'It wasn't me, Nazeem. I wasn't near your school yesterday.'

'I know you when I see you. And you knew it was me.

113

Even though you were a way off. I called your name. "Katie!" I shouted. And you turned right round.'

'It wasn't me, Nazeem!' Katie insisted. But Nazeem wouldn't listen.

'It was too. You were wearing a green anorak, and I must say, Katie, your hair looked absolutely filthy. As if you hadn't washed it in ages.' She took a deep, offended breath. 'And you turned right round, and you looked at me. And I waved . . . and then you ran . . . you ran away from me, Katie.'

She pouted, waiting for an apology.

Katie looked thoughtful. She knew what had happened. It had been Zan. And then Katie smiled.

'I don't know what's so funny, Katie. Why are you smiling like that?'

'Because you're wonderful, Nazeem.'

And she was.

And because, suddenly, Katie knew exactly how she was going to get rid of Mr Whittaker for good.

CHAPTER TEN

'You want your clothes back!' Zan obviously couldn't believe her ears. 'Some charity this is. I hope you get fleas!'

Katie handed her a black bin bag she'd been carrying. 'Here. I brought you more.'

'I haven't got a wardrobe, you know. Where am I supposed to keep all these?'

'You've been seen, Zan.'

She heard Zan catch her breath. 'That wee Nazeem, wasn't it? I thought she was going to chase me.'

'She thought you were me,' Katie said, her excitement mounting. 'She really thought you were me. Nazeem, who sees me almost every day. She makes sure of it.'

'So?' Zan was baffled.

Maybe, just maybe, Katie thought, she was as bright as Zan. She just hadn't had the need to use her wits

115

before. Necessity was, after all, the mother of brilliant ideas.

'So . . .?' Zan urged impatiently. 'Are you going to tell me? Or are you just going to sit there looking pleased with yourself all day?'

'You're going to let yourself be seen, over the next couple of days . . . like that . . .' She indicated the green anorak and jeans.

'You've got to be joking!' Zan was horrified. 'Your dad's vultures are everywhere. Forcing shelter and soup and fresh clothes on people, whether they want them or not.'

'That's exactly why some of them have to see you. You won't get caught and you're good at hiding. You told me that yourself.'

Zan threw her head back proudly. 'The best!'

'And you're good at running too.'

'Of course I am.'

'But I'm not. I'm going to get caught.'

Zan still looked puzzled.

'Don't you see? Over the next few days you're spotted. Word gets back to Whittaker – and it will – and on Friday, I'll swap clothes with you. I'll be the girl in the green anorak. And when they run after me . . . I'll be caught. I can't run for toffee.'

'Why Friday?'

'Because on Friday, Dad is supervising the soup kitchen at Hill Street. Mr Whittaker is going to be there with him. I heard him tell Mum. Both of them will catch me dressed as you – they couldn't not believe me after that!'

'And you think he'll fall for that?' The idea appealed to Zan, Katie could tell by the enthusiastic way she asked the question.

'I think he might. He believes there's someone, and that someone is always linked to me. Everyone he talks to tells him it's me, one and the same. All he needs is one final wee push, and I think he'll believe it's me too.'

Zan was still not completely convinced. 'And what excuse are you going to give your dad for running about in old clothes and condemned houses?'

'I've already thought about that. I'll tell him I managed to beat Ivy, and she made up the story about the other girl because she was so mortified that wee Katie Cassidy had got one over on her. So I thought if I dressed up like her they'd all believe it and leave me alone.'

Lies, lies and more lies, she heard her father's voice somewhere accusing her, and she felt guilty. She pushed the guilt away. It was for a good cause. The best.

'And he'll believe that?'

'As long as Mr Whittaker believes it, that's all that matters.'

Zan considered it all thoughtfully. Katie shivered. It was bitterly cold in the derelict flat Zan now called home. She had furnished one corner with a new card-board box, lined with an old blanket. Home. Katie shivered again. How could she sleep here?

Safer than anywhere else she'd been, she'd told Katie. Safer? Here? Where have you been, Zan?

'OK!' Zan slapped her knees. 'We'll give it a try. I'm in the mood for a wee bit of excitement anyway.'

On Wednesday her father told her that a girl had been seen on the dump. Just a glimpse, but enough to give Mr Whittaker some hope that he was on the right trail at last.

'What do you think of that?' her father asked, looking for some sign of guilt. He didn't have to look very far. Katie couldn't hide her blush. 'You said there was no girl. Remember?'

'Maybe it's a different girl. I've not seen her. How should I know?'

His eyes narrowed. He was annoyed with her. He began to say something else, then he changed his mind. He didn't understand. She knew that.

Things began to happen at school too. Katie was walking along the corridor when she was stopped by Mr Percy.

'Ah, Katie,' Mr Percy said. 'I've been thinking over your suggestion. Self-defence classes, remember?'

Of course she remembered. Silly question.

'I've been taking a survey, and it's a very popular idea. Good for young women to be able to take care of themselves. Even if there isn't a problem with bullies in this school.' He paused. His eyes never left hers. She had a feeling he had been talking to Miss Withers.

Katie smiled back at him. 'I think it's a great idea, sir.'

'I won't be starting them till after the Christmas break. In January. Sound all right?'

Christmas. Only a few weeks away. What would have happened by then?

'However . . . I do have another little idea I thought we might talk about.'

'We?' Katie said in surprise. 'You and me, sir?'

'Yes. You and me, Katie. I haven't time to talk about it

now. But I'll get back to you.' Then he was bounding off down the corridor to his next class.

'I wonder what his idea is?' she thought. And Mr Percy wanted to talk to *her* about it. Little Katie Cassidy?

She was ensconced in her room with Nazeem when her mother appeared.

'I'm off to my meeting, Katie. Now, Nazeem, you're sure your father's going to pick you up?'

'Oh yes, Mrs Cassidy.'

'Where's Dad?' Katie asked as her mother was closing the door.

'He's gone with Mr Whittaker to speak to someone who caught sight of that girl on the dump.'

When her mother had gone, Nazeem asked, 'Don't your mum and dad know that's you?'

Katie didn't quite know how to answer that one, but she didn't have to worry. Nazeem answered it herself. 'They probably wouldn't believe you anyway. Parents don't believe in magic.' She bounced up and down on the bed. Katie wondered how her bed survived it. 'Oh, this is fun. I wish we could have a sleepover.' Suddenly her eyes widened as if she'd just had a brilliant idea.

'Let's have one on Friday night! Mother's always saying I should have friends to sleep over. Will you come, Katie? Friday night?'

'I don't think I'll be able to.' Somehow, Katie had a feeling by Friday night she'd be grounded.

'But why not?' Nazeem waited for an answer. Katie hesitated, not quite sure how to answer her. She needn't have worried. Nazeem supplied her own answer.

'You're going to help someone, aren't you. The way you helped me?'

'I'm not going to be able to come to your house, Nazeem.'

Nazeem nodded enthusiastically. 'I understand. Don't worry. Your secret's safe with me.' She paused. 'You wouldn't mind if I had some other friends over to stay?'

'Of course I wouldn't,' Katie assured her.

'Friday is going to be just great!' screamed Nazeem excitedly.

Friday, thought Katie, is going to be a very important day for us all.

CHAPTER ELEVEN

Were they never going to spot her? Katie had been sitting here at the corner of Hill Street for half an hour. Her bottom was frozen and she was fed up. She'd been so sure someone would have seen her and passed the message on to her father and Mr Whittaker at the Community Hall. That is, until one old man on his way there stopped and whispered, 'Don't worry, dearie. I won't say a word.' He put a black-fingernailed hand across his whiskered mouth. 'Not a word.'

They were loyal, these people of the streets. They knew Zan didn't want to be found. They thought she was Zan. She would have to do something else. She'd have to go nearer, though she didn't want to. She wanted at least to give them a run for their money, and she reminded herself: she couldn't run for toffee.

She struggled to her feet. It was icy underfoot and she

almost slipped. She was going to run in this? What was she doing here? You're daft, Katie Cassidy, she told herself. Daft as a brush.

She trudged towards the Community Hall. People were going in, people were coming out. She hardly looked. She didn't think anyone was going to notice her anyway, or tell on her if they did. It had been a stupid, useless plan.

Then a man appeared in the doorway. A long, thin man. He leaned against the door smoking a cigarette, looking up and down the street. Katie froze. She actually froze. She couldn't move. She wouldn't be able to run. Now she knew what they meant when they said 'paralysed with fear'. Something about Mr Whittaker frightened her more than she could explain. She knew she had to get away from him. She took a deep breath. 'I've run away from Ivy Toner,' she told herself. 'This is going to be a dawdle.' She just wished she could believe that.

His eyes swept the street. At last, he saw her. He threw the cigarette away. His body tensed. Katie turned from him. She could move! She could run!

'Hey you, girl!'

Good. He hadn't recognized her as Katie. Not yet. She began to run and heard his footsteps behind her, too close. She put on an extra spurt, breathless already. I'll never keep this up. She could hear others joining in the chase.

'Stop!'

'We won't hurt you!'

'Come back. We don't mean you any harm.'

Still she ran. Katie never knew she could run like this. Like the wind. Like Zan.

She heard a startled cry behind her and glanced back. Mr Whittaker had gone flying on a patch of ice. A couple behind him, too late to stop, stumbled on top of him. It was comical, but she didn't have time to laugh. For suddenly, she could see her father, weaving in and out, catching up on them all. She turned and raced on.

Her legs were growing weak now. Her heart pounding. Any time now, she would have to stop. They would catch her.

She turned a corner, and was grabbed! 'Got you!' It was a woman, pinning Katie against her. 'I've got her! I've got her!' Katie pummelled her fists against the woman, tried to push her away, but the woman was stronger. 'You silly wee fool,' she said. 'We only want to help you.'

Then Mr Whittaker bounded round the corner and

grabbed her shoulders. His fingers bit into Katie's arms painfully. Why was he being so rough if he only wanted to help her? She struggled as he turned her round to face him.

'You!' His eyes blazed with anger. His grip tightened even more. For a moment Katie was sure he was going to slap her. She swallowed. She had never felt so much like fainting in her life. Then her father appeared. He took one look at Katie and his face drained of all its colour.

'Katie!' he said, and there was shock and surprise and disappointment just in the way he said it. 'Katie.'

'I thought it would keep Ivy Toner from bothering me. That's why I did it.'

She had tried to explain a dozen times to them, but the faces glowering back at her had no understanding in them.

'What a terrible trick to play on your father,' one woman said, her eyes cold and accusing.

'I did try to tell you, Dad. But you wouldn't believe me.'

He looked at her for a long time. 'I still don't understand, Katie.' He turned to Mr Whittaker. 'It looks as though those crazy stories are true. Katie and this girl . . . well, there is no other girl, is there?' Katie caught sight of herself in an old mirror lying askew against the wall. She looked tiny and vulnerable, not tough and strong the way Zan would look. She could almost see her reflection shimmer until Zan was looking back at her. Sitting up straight, defiance in her face, ready to run at the first opportunity. Let's face it, Katie told herself, Zan wouldn't even have got caught.

She was cold. So cold. There was tea being dished out to all and sundry. People were standing around her warming their hands round steaming mugs. No one had offered her anything yet and she didn't think they ever would.

'It looks as if I'm wasting my time here,' Mr Whittaker said at last.

Katie almost jumped to her feet in delight. It had worked! He was going. Zan could stay. That was worth everything. She'd make it up to her parents, all these lies. She made a promise right then. 'I will never lie again. I will devote the rest of my life to doing good works for the homeless.' Working with her father in Community Halls all over the country . . . the world even. She saw herself as a sort of Mother Teresa. A living saint. Receiving the Nobel Prize for Peace while her adoring mother and father looked on. She was going to make them proud of her.

'Well, I'm going to take this one home,' her father said, lifting her to her feet.

'And give her a good walloping when you get there, Douglas,' some charitable soul suggested.

Ha! Katie had never had a walloping in her life, and her father wasn't going to start now. At least . . . she hoped he wasn't.

'I've got an advert running in tonight's paper,' Mr Whittaker said. 'Too late to stop it. I suppose.'

Katie's ears pricked up.

'An advert?' her father asked.

'The usual thing . . . if anyone knows of the where-abouts, etc. I'll probably be inundated with letters telling me your daughter is the one I'm looking for.' His cold eyes fell again on Katie, all pretence of a smile gone. 'Wish I hadn't offered a reward.'

Katie was relieved. At last, Mr Whittaker would be out of their lives in a few days.

Katie couldn't wait to tell Zan, but how she was going to contact her she didn't know. She was grounded. The ninety-nine years her father had first suggested had been commuted by her mother to a month. Until Christmas. She was allowed out to go to school, and that was it. She was given half an hour to get home every day. Her father refused to speak to her, and even her mother was dry with her. She knew they were growing more distant every day, yet she couldn't do anything about it.

Still, Katie didn't despair. She had done what she had to do to help Zan. If she could explain to them, they would approve. She knew they would. And Christmas was coming. She loved Christmas. Her parents would relent. They would have parties and fun and laughter. How she wanted Zan to share in it all. If only, she thought, Zan could be with them for Christmas.

'Can I see you at break, Katie?' Mr Percy asked.

'Yes sir. What about, sir?'

He waved an answer away. 'I'll see you in my room by the gym, Katie,' he said, hurrying off.

What could he want her for? That 'idea' of his? Or did he know about Friday? Certainly everyone else in the school did. There had been delight that what they had always believed had finally been proved to be true. There was anger from Miss Withers. Silent anger, and looks that could kill. And there was confrontation with Ivy.

She was standing in a corner of the corridor as Katie hurried to Mr Percy's room later that day. She was trying to hide the cigarette she was smoking, but as Katie approached the smell from her breath alone would have given her away.

Katie took a deep breath and tried to hurry past her.

'Think you've fooled everybody, don't ye?' Ivy began to follow behind her. 'But I know this other lassie's here. I know it. And I'm goin' to prove it.'

Katie turned. Only a step away from Mr Percy's room. Safe to be brave, she decided. 'Go on then. Prove it.' She threw the words at her like a challenge. Ivy was too stupid to prove anything. She and Zan were much too smart for her.

Ivy flicked the lit cigarette at Katie angrily. 'I'm gonny. You better believe it!'

Katie was still shaking as she knocked on Mr Percy's door. Still afraid of Ivy. The habit of a lifetime dies hard.

'Come in, Katie.'

He pointed her to a chair and she sat down. He began to stride about the room. He was wearing the school football strip, with a whistle strung round his neck, and he looked slightly ridiculous. 'So, I believe you just suddenly turn yourself into a kind of Superwoman character . . . is that right?' Was he making a fool of her? She was sure he was.

'OK, that's your business,' he said, when she made no reply. 'What I want to talk about is this. You and I both know bullying goes on in this school. How do we get to the root of the problem, Katie? You've suffered. I think you've thought about it. That's why you suggested self-defence classes. So . . . what else can we do?'

She couldn't believe it. He was asking her for advice?

'First,' she said, 'I'd make sure every child who complained about bullying was believed. Too often you're told, "Oh, but we need proof of that."'

'But that's true, we have to have proof.'

'But they're fly, bullies. They will always wait till nobody's there. Till you're alone. And you have no witnesses. It should be looked into at the first complaint . . . bullies never do it just the once. They always have a reputation for bullying – why should you need so much proof? I'd give them only three warnings, their parents should be told, and then they'd be out.'

'Don't you think, Katie, that to get to the root of the trouble we should perhaps be finding out why these pupils find it necessary to bully in the first place? They probably have problems at home . . . If we could . . . if we could find out what these problems are . . . help them . . . Where are you going, Katie?'

Katie was heading for the door. 'Did you listen to what you just said, sir? You've turned it round. Teachers always do. Instead of worrying about the child who is being bullied, they start worrying about the bully.'

'I didn't mean . . .'

'That's why it'll never be solved, sir, because the first priority is never the child who's being bullied. Why don't you try to protect the pupils in danger first? You could form a committee of older pupils. To look after new pupils, especially the ones who are different . . .' she thought of little Nazeem, '. . . the ones no one else wants to be friendly with.' She thought of Teresa Henderson. 'Bullies only pick on the weakest. They can't get you if you've got friends. And sometimes your friends desert you because they're frightened too, and they're so glad it's not them that's being picked on. But if there was a group of older pupils you knew you could go to, who would never desert you, do you know how much that would mean, sir? When you're just all alone and you've got nobody to turn to.' She was reliving all those weeks and months when she had lived in fear of going to school.

'Do you not think you're being a wee bit unfair, Katie? The teachers are always here to help.'

'The teachers!' Katie was almost ready to cry. 'Do you know, sir, the day Ivy Toner shoved my head down the lavatory pan . . .' The tears began to fall now, as she remembered the shame, the humiliation. She could see herself now, hurtling along the corridor. 'I ran to Miss Withers, she was our class teacher, and do you know what she said, sir . . .?'

Mr Percy looked upset. She knew her tears were upsetting him. Well, let them!

'Do you know what she said, sir?' she repeated. 'She said . . . "Poor Ivy . . . she must have some terrible problems at home if she's resorting to this kind of behaviour!"'

Katie didn't wait for his reaction. She flung open the door and slammed straight into Miss Withers herself. She was ashen-faced with anger. She had heard everything, and Katie didn't care.

'Yes, you did, Miss. You did!' And she ran, her feet clattering down the corridor.

I'll be expelled, she thought as she made her way home.

That's OK. I'll be sent to the posh school, Riverside Academy. Mum's always wanted me to go there. No, I won't, she decided. They'd never risk sending me there. No. It's borstal for me.

It seemed no matter how hard she tried to solve her problems, she just entangled them more and more about her.

She was almost glad to be home. She went straight to her room and lay down on the bed. She tried to think of all the good things that were happening. She had helped Zan. Mr Whittaker would be leaving soon. Mr Percy really wanted to help, or at least he had until her outburst . . . Nothing helped. The black mood brought on by the memories of all she had been through, all she had suffered from Ivy, just wouldn't lift. It just wasn't fair. The distance between herself and her parents was widening every day. She felt more alone than she ever had, except for Zan. Why couldn't her parents understand? Why couldn't they trust her?

She heard the phone ring faintly, and her mother answer it. Then her father's strident voice calling her made her jump. It was not a friendly call. 'KATIE! COME DOWN HERE RIGHT NOW!'

Oh, no, she thought, what had she done now?

Her father was at the bottom of the stairs glaring up at her as she came down. Her mother looked just as angry, but puzzled too. Suddenly, Katie had had enough. She wasn't going to be little Katie with tears in her eyes, wanting them to understand. She was going to stand up to them. She'd done nothing to be ashamed of. She lifted her head high. 'So?' she asked. 'What am I blamed for this time?'

Her father's eyes flashed. 'Don't you take that tone with me, girl.'

'That's just the attitude that's causing all the problems,' her mother said.

'What do you mean?'

'That was Miss Withers on the phone,' her father told her through gritted teeth. 'She wants us to come in to the school tomorrow to discuss . . . your deteriorating attitude. It seems you were quite the little madam today at school.'

'We always brought you up to respect your teachers!' her mother snapped.

Katie looked from one to the other. 'I don't believe this,' she said. 'All I did was tell the truth. Miss Withers didn't like it, so she calls you. Did Ivy Toner's parents ever get a call like that from Miss Withers, I wonder?'

'Maybe the difference is that Ivy Toner's parents didn't care. We do. What is happening, Katie?'

'I wouldn't do anything bad, Dad. You know that.'

'I don't know anything any more,' her father said. 'All these lies. You're changing Katie. Everyone sees it. You expect us to trust you. Why don't you trust us? Tell us what's going on?'

Katie hesitated. She wanted to tell them everything at that moment. Sure enough of them that they would protect Zan, just as she was. Or would they? Their help would mean discovery for Zan. It would mean Mr Whittaker finding her, even if he might eliminate her as the girl he was looking for. It would mean betraying Zan. Breaking her promise. She couldn't do that.

Her father's patience was wearing thin. 'This is your last chance to tell the truth. What's going on, Katie?'

It was a dilemma and she couldn't see a way out of it. She pushed her knuckles into her mouth and bit them. She couldn't tell. She couldn't.

She'd never seen that look in her father's eyes before. Disgust, anger, disappointment. 'I don't know you any more,' he said bitterly. Then he turned from her. 'Get out of my sight. If I never see you again, it'll be too soon!'

Katie gasped. Even her mother was shocked. 'Douglas!'

'That's OK by me!' Katie screamed. 'I hope I never see you again. Either of you!'

She ran up to her room and cried for a long time. She'd show them. They didn't trust her? They didn't believe anything she said? Fine. She was fed up with them, and with living by their rules and regulations.

Look at Zan. Her own boss. She'd done all right without her parents. Living rough. No one told her what to do. Well, she could be like Zan. No one was ever going to tell her what to do again. She and Zan. Together. Life would be an adventure. She saw herself leaving this town. Leaving all her troubles behind her. It was the only way out. She was enmeshed in so many lies, and to tell the truth about Zan was the only way out. She could never do that. No. Life on the road with Zan was the only freedom.

She sat up and wiped the tears from her eyes. A decision made. Her dad didn't want to see her again? Well, he wouldn't have to. She was going to run away. With Zan!

CHAPTER TWELVE

Katie had never been so terrified in all her life. Had Zan moved? This had been her place. In the cardboard box in a corner of this old tenement flat. Tonight, in midnight blackness, she had tiptoed in and shaken the figure sleeping there.

It hadn't been Zan. Instead, an old man with a grey beard that looked as if he kept his next meal in it had turned a bleary, puzzled eye on her. Katie screamed and jumped back. The old man did the same.

'This is Zan's place,' Katie said. 'A girl. She lives here.'

'This is my place!' he said gruffly. 'My place!'

Katie stood in the mouth of the derelict close, freezing with cold and fear. It was pouring with icy rain. What a night to decide to leave home! She sat on her case and tried to think what to do next. If she couldn't find Zan, she would sleep herself in one of these old empty closes. Herself. The word echoed in her mind. herself. Alone. In the cold. In the dark. She shivered. She must find Zan! But where?

She had never felt this cold, or this frightened. Then she remembered Ivy, and knew she had. Things had been worse than this. Not a lot. But they had been worse.

What would she do if she couldn't find Zan? Perhaps she had left town after all. No! She wouldn't do that. Not without telling Katie. She was good at hiding. Hadn't she always told Katie that? Zan was hiding somewhere. All Katie had to do was find her.

One thing she couldn't do was go home. She'd never go home again. Her parents didn't really care about her. They didn't believe in her. She saw herself years from now when she was old, twenty maybe, returning to her aged mother and father. She could picture them, her father with his zimmer, her mother knitting in a rocking-chair by the fire. First she would have to learn to knit, of course, but that was probably something you picked up as you got on in years. Katie would only return then. Successful and famous for all her good works. One of those newspapers that always had pictures of naked women in them had just run a story, 'The Angel of Mercy'. That would be Katie. It would tell of how she'd had to leave home because her parents didn't trust her. They thought she was bad. Because of that story they had received hate mail, and threatening letters. So Katie had returned, to assure them she held no grudges. They had ruined her young life, destroyed her childhood, but she forgave them!

Yes, she could see it all.

'What are you doing here!'

Heart attack time! Katie almost fainted. It was Zan!

'Where have you moved to? I've been looking for you!'

'I've found a great place.'

'Where?'

'An old warehouse on the edge of town.'

Katie knew exactly where she meant. 'But that's falling to bits. It's dangerous. No one ever goes near there . . .'

'I know,' Zan said triumphantly. 'Perfect!'

'So why did you move?'

'Never stay anywhere too long. Safer to move. What are you doing here?'

Quickly, Katie told her story.

'So,' Zan said when she'd finished, 'you've left home?'

Katie held up her suitcase. 'Why do you think I brought this?' Zan began to laugh as if she'd never stop.

Katie was a little annoyed. 'What's so funny?'

'You run away from home. You're going to live rough. And you bring luggage! What have you got in there, your hairdrier?'

She was very glad Zan couldn't see her red face in the darkness of the close. That was exactly what she had brought. And her mousse and deodorant. And lots and lots of clean underwear.

'What did you come back for?' Katie asked.

Zan held up an old cracked alarm clock. 'It's mine!' she said possessively. 'Forgot it. I wasn't leaving it for him.' She gestured up to where the old tramp lay sleeping. 'Come on, let's go home. Have you eaten?'

Katie shook her head.

'Bring any food?'

'I didn't think.'

Zan threw up her hands in despair. 'You didn't think! You'll have to start thinking if you're going to live rough. Come on, I've got something. We'll have to run.' She pulled Katie to her feet. 'That rain's not going to let up.'

No matter how fast they ran, and in Katie's case that

wasn't very fast, they were still drenched by the time they reached the old warehouse. It was silhouetted against the lights from the town, and reminded Katie of something out of a horror movie.

'Aren't you ever afraid living in places like this?'

'Sometimes there's things a lot scarier. Come on, I'm up here.'

'Up here' was a long shaky metal ladder hanging from a platform high in the loft. Katie froze, but Zan rose like a monkey.

'Why on earth do you have to be away up there?' Katie called after her.

'It's safer. And warmer. Come on up.'

One rung at a time, Katie climbed. If only she didn't have this daft case. If only she hadn't worn so many clothes. If only she wasn't a total dimwit, she wouldn't be here in the first place.

'Hand me the case.' Zan's face peered over the platform, her hand extended. Katie was too frightened to look up. To look down. To move. Shaking, she passed the case up to Zan. 'One more step and you're here!'

Katie collapsed on to the platform. 'I'm never going to leave here. I'm going to grow old here, and I'm going to die here.'

Zan fell about laughing. 'Of hunger probably,' she said through a giggle. 'Here, look what I've got.' She plunged her hand inside her anorak and brought out a fish supper. Squashed and cold.

'I wondered what the smell was,' Katie said. 'Where did you get the money for that?' Zan looked at her blankly. 'You didn't steal it?' Katie could never eat stolen property, she decided. No matter how hungry she was.

'Of course I didn't steal it.' Zan sounded affronted. Then she added. 'Not this time. Someone threw it away.'

This was even worse than stealing it!

'People do that all the time,' Zan continued. 'They waste so much. Eat a couple of chips, then throw it down. Well seen they've never been really hungry.'

'You took it out of a bin?'

'It's all right. It's fresh made. Look, there's two pieces of fish. Have one.' She held out a squashed battered haddock to Katie. Katie shrank back.

Zan shrugged. 'Please yourself. Fish is very good for you. Gives you brains. Though I always think if they were so smart they wouldn't get caught in the first place, would they?' She popped a piece of fish in her mouth.

'I don't know how you could eat that,' Katie said.

'Because I'm hungry, Katie. And when you're hungry and homeless, you'll eat anything.'

Katie thought she'd draw the line at cold fish suppers.

Zan leaned towards her. 'You've seen homeless people picking through litter bins looking for scraps of food.'

Katie nodded. 'Of course.'

'You think that's the way they like to eat? They're desperate, Katie. Starving. You'd die if I told you some of the things I've eaten.'

'I don't think I want to know.'

'You'll eat them too, if you come on the road with me.'

'I never will,' Katie said with assurance.

'That's what I said too,' Zan replied. 'But you'll do a lot of things. You have to. Just to survive. Begging's the worst.'

'I'll never beg!' Katie said at once.

'There you go again. But you will. And you'll hate it. People walking past you with their noses in the air.' Zan's voice grew thoughtful. 'There's some people generous, especially when you're young, like me. But there's always someone who takes too much interest. Wants to help too much, contact social services . . . and I have to run again.' It was as if Zan was talking to herself now. Remembering with shame those moments.

Katie was thinking she wasn't going to be very good at this kind of life.

'What's that noise?' She jumped. Someone was in the loft with them. Rain battered against the broken roof, drips splashed on to the floor below them. Here on the platform they were dry.

'I'm not the only one who knows this is a good place to be.'

'You share this with someone else?' In a second she knew who that someone else was. A rat suddenly scurried along a beam behind them. Katie screamed and stood up. Zan laughed.

'They're more afraid of you than you are of them.'

Katie sat down again and wrapped her arms around herself. 'How can you bear it, Zan?'

Zan lay back against some old sacking dreamily. 'Didn't think I'd ever get used to it. There were nights I'd lie so cold, so hungry . . .'

'Why didn't you just go home?'

Zan took a while to answer. 'Maybe I had no home to go to.'

'Why don't you ever answer my questions? You can trust me, you know that.'

'It wouldn't do you, or me, any good if I told you.'

'I'm so cold, Zan.' Katie wanted to cry, but couldn't. Katie lived like this all the time. She'd only been on the road two hours and she'd already had enough.

'And you'll get colder and hungrier. It's not an adventure living like this. No one does it because they want to.'

'I don't want to either,' Katie said. 'I have to. My dad said he never wanted to see me again.'

'He didn't mean that.'

'You're sticking up for my dad?'

'You've been lying to him. How's he supposed to feel? And it's all my fault. You've had nothing but trouble since you met me, Katie. Maybe I didn't help you at all.'

'Don't ever say that,' Katie said at once. 'You did. I tell you, Zan . . . you're the best thing that ever happened to me.'

Zan was inordinately pleased. 'Goodness, I've never been the best thing that happened to anyone before.' The girls smiled at each other, and there, high in the cold dark warehouse, all worries were forgotten for a moment.

'I never really thanked you for what you did for me, Katie.'

'I was only paying you back. We're even now.'

145

'You're the best friend I've ever had.' Zan said as if it was the hardest thing she'd ever had to do.

Katie grinned. 'I'm the only friend you've ever had.'

'Yes. I forgot.' That set them both laughing again. Their laughter echoing eerily through the warehouse. Then, suddenly, Zan was serious again. 'You don't really want to run away. Your mother and father care about you. You know that. They're good people.'

'You said my dad is a typical do-gooder.'

'He is. But at least he's trying to do something to help homeless people. I hear them talking. He's trying to find some of them real homes in the town.'

'You could live in a real home, Zan. In fact, you could come and live with me. My mum and dad would adopt you. We could be like sisters. I'll go back home if you come with me. You're all the proof I need. Come home with me, Zan.'

For a moment Zan said nothing. Katie could make out her face, thoughtful, thinking over everything Katie had said. Was she thinking the same thing as Katie, seeing the same pictures? The two of them sharing a bedroom, laughing, having fun, going on family holidays in the Algarve, like sisters. Like twins. And even in the dark Katie could see Zan's eyes fill with tears. Zan crying? It was unbelievable.

'Can't ever be, Katie. I'll always have to hide. Don't ask me to explain.'

'Then I'll never leave you,' Katie said with determination.

Zan sniffed and wiped her grimy face with her sleeve. 'You're going home,' she said. 'You know you are.'

And Katie knew she was right. She wasn't cut out for this. She would just have to go back and face up to everything.

'I'll be in even more trouble when I go back,' she groaned.

'Sometimes,' Zan said, 'it takes even more courage to go back.'

Once more a police car was sitting outside her house when she turned into her street. It was almost four in the morning. Zan had come with her to the corner, and gave her an encouraging push. 'Go on,' she said. 'You can do it.'

As she pushed open the front door they all turned to stare at her. Her dad, her mum, and those same two policemen, Blue-eyes and Ginger. Her parents ran and scooped her up in their arms.

'Oh, Katie, Katie, where have you been? I've been so worried,' her mother said, crying.

'Don't ever do that again.' There was pain in her father's voice, and worry. He hadn't understood before, and he understood even less now. But he looked drawn and pale with worry about her. Nothing had changed. She still couldn't tell the truth. They still didn't understand. Yet she knew she would never run away again. Here was where she belonged.

She was safely tucked up in bed, snug and warm, before she cried. She cried for Zan sitting high in the old warehouse with the rats, neither snug nor warm. Her mother came into the room, saw her tears and ran to her.

'Don't cry.' She hugged her close. 'You're back and that's all that matters. Your father has been so upset. And you can't blame him, Katie. He's so worried.'

'Worried I might spoil his chances for re-election?'

She felt her mother tense. 'Don't say that! You know it isn't true. We were worried sick you might have gone off with this other girl.'

This time it was Katie who tensed. 'But . . . there is no other girl. Remember?'

'Perhaps you don't know her, but there is another girl. Mr Whittaker had an answer to his advert. Someone can prove she does exist and that she's living here in town.'

Katie's heart pounded. Not this. Not now.

'He came tonight to tell us. And when we found you were gone . . . oh . . .'

'But why should you be so worried? I don't know this girl.'

'He said he hadn't been able to tell us before. Still couldn't tell the police. Just in case this isn't the girl he's looking for. But in the circumstances . . . you gone . . . he'd break the rule just for us. We were so afraid for you.'

'Afraid? I don't understand. What did he say?'

Her mother pulled her tighter against her, and it was a moment before she spoke. 'This girl is dangerous, Katie. She burned down her house, while her parents were asleep inside! They died, Katie! They died!'

CHAPTER THIRTEEN

Katie wouldn't believe it. She tossed and turned during all that was left of the night, and she still wouldn't believe it. Yet it explained so much. Why Zan would never talk of her past. Why she could never go back. But Zan . . . do anything so horrific? No. If no one else would believe her, Katie would. Always. The girl Mr Whittaker was looking for had to be someone else.

So someone had answered his advert.

Who?

She awoke to the smell of smoked bacon and eggs wafting up from the kitchen. Her mother was singing out of tune along with Whitney Houston. What was Zan waking up to, high up in her loft? Pigeons nesting in the roof, rats scuttling along creaky old beams. The remnants of a cold fish supper for breakfast. Katie shivered, glad she was home. With all her problems, so glad to be warm and safe again.

'Your father's still not talking to you,' her mother informed her as she plated her ham and eggs. 'He wanted me to get you up for school. Don't think because I didn't, that I'm pleased with you either.' Her mother's relief at her safe return had been replaced by anger at her going in the first place. 'I mean, running away, Katie! Haven't we taught you anything? Running away never solves anything.'

That's what Zan had done, run away, Katie thought. Had it solved anything for her?

'The girl Mr Whittaker's looking for,' Katie asked later. 'How does he know she did . . . that . . .' She couldn't bring herself to say it.

'It happened over a year ago. He's been on her trail ever since. Even the police have given up looking.'

'So why is he still?'

'His clients are the girl's family. An aunt and uncle. They know she needs treatment. They want her found, cared for.'

'She'd be put away.'

Zan without her freedom. Unthinkable.

'Until she's better. Look. Katie, do you know any-thing about this girl?'

Katie shook her head quickly. 'No. Honest.' And knew it sounded like the lie it was.

'She's dangerous. Can't you understand that!'

'Why would anyone do such a terrible thing?'

'She was always a problem child. Always running away. Resented her parents. The wee girl's probably sick in the mind. She needs help. If you know anything, Katie . . .'

'I don't. I told you.'

Her mother shrugged. 'Oh, well, they'll find her. Don't you worry. She won't be able to hide for long.'

She had to help Zan get away. She had to warn her. Most of all, she had to ask her for the truth. The truth at last. But how?

As if reading her thoughts, her mother said, 'You're still grounded, remember. You're staying in all day. And so am I, just to make sure.'

Katie couldn't settle herself all day. The net was closing in on Zan and *she* was sitting about the house helplessly. She comforted herself that they'd never find Zan in the warehouse. From her lofty vantage point she could spot any danger. If only she could get out of the house to warn her.

*

It was four o'clock and the door was being pounded as if someone was trying to break in. When her mother didn't answer at once Katie glanced out of her window and saw that she was at the back of the garden chatting over the fence to the woman next door. Katie hurried downstairs. Nazeem almost fell into the hallway as she pulled open the door. Breathlessly, she struggled to get up.

'She told me to tell you . . .' Nazeem began – she could still hardly catch her breath. She looked as if she had run all the way there.

'Tell me what?' Katie said. 'Who? What are you talking about?'

'Ivy!' Nazeem's voice was almost a scream. 'Ivy told me . . .' Katie could see she was trying to remember the exact words. 'She said . . . she'd got you. At last. She's found out where Zan is. She answered Mr Whittaker's advert, and she's going to take him there. Oh, Katie, that's that nasty man with the face.'

Katie was trying to take all this in.

'And they're going to catch her. And you can't do anything to stop her, 'cause you're grounded. And nobody would believe you anyway.' Nazeem took a deep breath. 'And she said to tell you, she'd won.'

Ivy knew where Zan was? But how? They were going

to trap her. How? Oh, what did it matter! Ivy knew, and soon so would Whittaker.

'But there isn't another girl. Katie. Zan is you. Everybody knows that.' Nazeem didn't sound so sure now. 'What are you going to do, Katie?'

Katie was too busy thinking to answer. She had to help Zan. Warn her. Ivy thought she'd won! Well, she'd show Ivy!

'I can't explain right now,' Katie said. 'You've got to trust me. I have to go.'

'But you're grounded, Katie,' Nazeem reminded her.

She called back as she ran down the path. 'Tell my mother . . . Oh, tell her something, will you?'

Nazeem shouted after her. 'What?'

'I don't know, think of something.'

And then she ran as she had never run before. Down the well-lit street, with Christmas trees lighting up the windows, past shops full of warmth and light. She ran into the empty streets, leaving the warmth and light behind. She ran into the blackness to warn Zan.

It was pitch black in the warehouse as Katie moved stealthily inside. 'Zan,' she called. 'Are you in there?'

There was a sudden movement from above. She

hoped it was Zan and not one of those blinking rats.

'Katie?' There was surprise in Zan's voice. 'What are you doing here? You're not running away again, I hope?'

'Zan. You're in trouble.'

It was hard calling up. Hard for Zan to hear. 'Best come up,' Zan said.

Up that ladder? Katie took a deep breath and began to climb.

'They're coming to get you.' She began to talk to take her mind off her fear. 'Ivy knows where you are. She's bringing Whittaker. Tonight. We have to hurry.'

'But how? How did she find out?'

'What does it matter? She knows. Just take what you can carry. Let's get out of here.'

'I . . . I can't get caught, Katie.' Something in the way she said it made Katie stop climbing and look up. Zan's face was grimy and unsmiling as she peered over the platform. She was reminded suddenly of the Zan she had first met on the dump. The one who had frightened her.

'She's dangerous.' Her mother's words rushed at her like a cold breath of wind.

'He said . . . you killed your mother and father.' Katie watched her expression. It didn't change.

'And do you believe that?'

'Why is it so important you're not caught then?' She had to know the truth. She had to.

'Don't make me remember,' Zan said softly.

'I have to know, Zan.'

It seemed an age before Zan answered. Katie forgot everything, where she was, how afraid she was, how much they needed to get away. There wasn't another sound in the warehouse, nothing except Katie's deep breaths and Zan's soft words when they came.

'They were bad to me, Katie, so bad. I kept running away. The police kept bringing me back. No one would believe me. I was the bad one. The troublemaker.'

Katie could understand that. Hadn't the same thing happened to her?

'I didn't burn the house down . . . you must believe that. My parents were mixed up with bad people, dangerous people. There'd been some kind of quarrel. They were scared, my parents, terrified. They took it out on me. The night it happened, I was running away again. But I didn't burn the house down. I could never do that, no matter how bad they were. But the police would never believe a child. A "bad" child like me. And I was too afraid to wait around to tell them the truth. They wouldn't have believed me anyway . . .'

'The truth . . .?'

'I saw him, Katie . . . the man who did burn the house down. And he saw me. He said he'd get me one day . . . I've been running ever since.'

'Who?' Katie asked.

'I'll never forget his face, Katie. The house was dark. They were sleeping upstairs . . . and I was sneaking out of the back door. I saw his shadow in the living-room. I stopped . . . and suddenly . . .' Zan drew in her breath sharply, reliving the moment '. . . suddenly he struck a match . . . and it lit up his face, his eyes . . . made them look so strange and eerie. I'll never forget it, Katie . . . those deep sunk eyes . . . that long thin dark face.'

CHAPTER FOURTEEN

Katie almost fell off the ladder! Zan grabbed her, clutching her sleeve just in time. 'Katie! What is it!'

Katie scrambled up the ladder, all fear of heights gone in an instant. She was breathless. 'Zan, this man! He's here! He's Whittaker!'

Even in the dark, Katie could see the colour drain from Zan's face. 'I should have known. I should have realized.'

'But why? Even my father thought he was genuine.'

Zan was already stuffing her pitiful belongings into a black bin bag. 'I have to get out of here!'

Katie began to help. 'I know, I know.' She could feel beads of sweat on her brow, feel her heart pounding inside her. She should have known too. Her gut feeling the very first time she saw him had told her there was something sinister about Whittaker. Why hadn't she listened to that little voice? Instead of all the common sense of her parents. Her parents were high on common sense – most grown-ups were. He has a licence, authority, therefore he must only have her best interests at heart. What a great cover for a man looking for someone! A private investigator, with clients whose confidence he had to keep.

'Oh, come on, Zan. Hurry!' Katie put one foot over the loft and froze once again. The ladder wasn't there!

'You're no' goin' anywhere, Cassidy!'

Zan shrank back against the wall. Katie looked down. Way below was Ivy, just discernible in a shaft of moonlight, and with her Lindy and Michelle and the Posse.

'You're dead easy to trick, d'you know that, Cassidy?' Katie could only just make out her grin. 'I knew you'd come runnin' to save your pal.'

Smarter than we gave her credit for, Katie thought.

'What pal? There's no one else here.' Her voice was shaky. But they couldn't possibly know Zan was up here with her. Katie pulled back from their view. 'They can't *know* you're here,' she whispered to Zan.

Zan nodded.

Katie called down again. 'I don't know what your plan was, but I'm up here by myself.' She said it with as much conviction as she could muster.

'Think I'm stupit? I know she's up there wi' you.'

No, you don't, Katie thought. You think she is. You believe she is. But you don't *know* she is. There was still a chance.

'Michelle!' Ivy ordered. 'You run and get Whi-aker.' She said his name as if it had no t's. Whi-aker.

Michelle laughed inanely, and the sound of her running footsteps moved off into the distance. Whittaker didn't know where Zan was. Not yet. No time to lose. Still a chance.

'I'll just keep yous up there till he comes, and see when he comes. Know whit he says . . .' Ivy was laughing already. Obviously they had discussed 'what he says' for a long time. 'Whi-aker says we can dae what we like wi' you. As long as he gets the other one.'

'He's going to be disappointed. There isn't another one up here.'

'Aye, there is so. So there is?'

Katie peered over the loft again. Ivy was looking round at the others. They all looked slightly baffled. They didn't know how to answer. There still a chance. A chance for Zan at least.

'See if that's right, Ivy,' one of the Posse was saying.

'That Whi-aker'll be really mad at us.'

'We'll no' get the reward.'

'Why don't you come up here and check?' Katie suggested.

Ivy's eyes widened in alarm. 'You've got to be jokin'. Think I'm stupit! I'm keepin' you up there till Whi-aker comes.'

'You're going to look stupid when he does come, and I'm up here alone.'

'I think you better check, Ivy.'

'She's kiddin' us on, can you no' see that?'

The others weren't so sure, and neither now was Ivy.

Zan pulled at Katie's sleeve. 'What are you doing?' she said, in a voice even softer than a whisper.

'If I can convince them I'm on my own . . . Mr Whittaker will stop looking for you. You'll have a chance to get away.'

'But you, Katie . . .' Zan clutched her sleeve tighter. 'You'd do that for me?'

'You have to get away, Zan,' Katie said.

'You're the bravest person I've ever met, Katie.'

'Me?' She didn't feel very brave. Actually, she was scared stiff. All she knew was that Zan had to escape from Whittaker. Zan was in even more danger than Katie.

'Can you hide up here?' Katie asked, her eyes searching round the platform. Old sacks in the corner, an old box pushed against a wall. 'Can you?' she repeated.

'Sure, I'm the best at hiding.' For the first time there was a smile in Zan's voice. 'You leave the hiding to me.'

Katie peered back down to where Ivy stood. 'I'll come down. Then if there is another one up here, you can keep her up here till Whittaker comes.'

Katie could see the fear in their eyes. As if they were afraid of her, of wee Katie Cassidy. They had hoped to keep her high up there till Whittaker came.

Lindy grabbed Ivy's shoulder. 'That makes sense, Ivy. We'll have Katie doon here and that other yin up there.'

Ivy shook herself free. 'I don't trust her.' She thought about it for a moment. 'A'right. Come on doon. But I'm goin' up there. I'll see where this other yin is.'

Katie turned to Zan. This might be the last time she would ever see her. She felt like crying. But it wasn't the time to cry. 'You be careful, Zan,'

Zan nodded. 'I'll miss you, Katie . . .'

They jumped at the sound of Ivy hooking the ladder against the platform. 'Right. Doon here, you!'

Katie put her foot over the loft and began to go down. She tried not to be afraid. ' 'Tis a far, far better thing that

I do' and all that. But she couldn't help shaking as she went down. She hoped they thought it was the ladder. Ivy and Lindy and the Posse were circled round her like vultures. Ivy grabbed her hair as soon as she stepped off the ladder. She pulled it back hard. Katie had to bite her lip to keep from crying out.

'Hang on to her!' she ordered and she passed Katie roughly to Lindy.

'You goin' up there?' Lindy asked.

Katie could see Ivy was afraid. She saw her swallow. 'Aye,' she said at last.

She climbed slowly, and the ladder shook even more than it had when Katie had been on it. Katie prayed. She prayed Zan had hidden well. But where? There was nowhere to hide. Finally, Ivy reached the top. She stood on the top rung, her eyes searching the platform.

'She must be here,' Katie heard her say. 'She's hiding.' Ivy climbed on to the platform. Katie held her breath. If Ivy searched for her she had to find her. Katie began to struggle. If she could run away, create some kind of diversion . . . but the three girls holding her were stronger than she was, and angrier than she could ever be.

Suddenly Ivy shouted out triumphantly. 'She's here! Under the sacks. I can see her moving. I've got her!'

Katie felt her legs turn to jelly. It's all over, she thought.

There was a sudden terrified scream. Ivy appeared at the top of the ladder and began to scramble down. 'Rats!' she was screaming. 'There's millions of rats up here!'

Rats! Katie realized with relief. They had been friendly after all.

'I told you she wasn't there,' Katie said when Ivy jumped from the bottom step.

Her face was red with anger. 'You're going to be sorry.' Ivy prodded Katie with her finger, pushing her back against the wall. Still held tight by Lindy, Katie started to struggle. If she could get out of here, Zan would have a chance to climb down the ladder and maybe, just maybe, she could sneak off and be safely away before Whittaker arrived. Ivy was pushing her hard and Lindy's fingers were biting into her arm. They were both stronger than she was. But not smarter, Katie reminded herself.

'The rats!' she shouted suddenly. 'Look, the rats!'

Ivy screamed and turned. Lindy let her go and bolted. Katie ran for all she was worth.

They were after her in an instant. They'd been tricked. And that realization made them angrier than ever. If Katie could just make it outside the warehouse! She darted this way and that. Someone leaped at her and she sidestepped them. They landed hard on the ground beside her. Someone pushed her, she stumbled. She fell. Ivy was on her, grabbing her ankles. Somehow Katie got to her feet. But by that time the others had surrounded her.

'Smart wee bitch!' one of them said.

' 'Mon we'll show her,' said another.

They were outside the warehouse, just. The moon cast eerie lights on the faces around Katie. At least, Zan could get away. Zan could be safe. Her relief at that was tinged with fear.

What were they going to do to her now?

Ivy's face was so close she spat the words at Katie. 'Thought you were that clever, didn't you? Thought you'd get away, didn't ye?'

'We're a' goin' to get you now.'

Katie closed her eyes. Nothing could save her now.

In that instant, there was a frightened yelp. Katie opened her eyes in time to see one of the Posse fall face down in the mud. The girl screamed. 'Something grabbed my ankle there!'

'Where?' Ivy's question became a croak as she was yanked back, her arms flailing, trying to keep her balance. Failing. She fell on her back. Splat! The rest of the group took a step back, their eyes darting all around. What was happening?

Katie knew. Divide and rule. Zan! That thought gave Katie the strength to struggle free. With as much power as she could find, she pushed them aside. Taken by surprise, they fell easily. Ivy scrambled to her feet, crouching. She grabbed for Katie. Katie sidestepped her. At the same moment, Ivy was caught by the ankles again. Again she went down with a frustrated scream. Katie caught sight of Zan's face in the moonlight. Triumphant.

'Run for it!' Zan mouthed.

Katie ran. Zan ran beside her. He who fights and runs away . . .

'Why?' Katie whispered as they ran. 'You could have got away!'

'Too many of them, kid. I couldn't leave you to that.'

Katie could hardly believe it. A few moments ago, all was lost. Now, they were free. Both of them. They had done it together. Again. She felt like whooping with joy. She glanced at Zan as they ran. She looked as delighted as Katie.

At that instant they both collided with someone, looming out of the dark, arms outstretched to bar their way.

'Going somewhere?'

It was Whittaker, with his low, sinister . . . oh, so sinister voice.

Katie had never seen Zan so afraid. He had her tight by the arm. Katie had to help her. Above everything, Zan had to get away from Whittaker! More in sheer fright than anything else, Katie bit hard into his hand. He screamed through his teeth, and for a split second released Zan to push Katie from him. It was all the time Zan needed. She was off like the wind. Whittaker drew in an angry breath. He threw Katie from him roughly, then he was after Zan. Katie lay there for a second, watching them both disappear into the pitch darkness of the warehouse.

'You're no' gonny get away this time, scunner.' Ivy, closing in on her. Katie shrank back. She tried to stand up. But Lindy stood on her hand, squashing it into the soft mud. Katie bit her lip. She wouldn't cry. No matter what they did.

Ivy grinned viciously. 'I'm goin' to enjoy kickin'

lumps out o' you.' She looked around. 'We all are, aren't we, lassies.'

No one knew where she was.

No one knew Zan existed.

It was hopeless praying for help.

Nothing could save her now!

CHAPTER FIFTEEN

Ivy lifted her foot, preparing for that first vicious kick. Katie closed her eyes, and prayed anyway.

'Don't you dare touch her!!!'

The words boomed into the cold night air. Somewhere a bird whooped up across the dark sky.

Katie gasped and opened one eye. Her father's voice? But how?

'You leave my wee girl alone!' Her mother! It was a miracle. The cavalry had arrived.

Ivy and her cohorts, mouths agape, took a few steps back. They couldn't believe it either.

'You leave my friend be!' Nazeem too?

Out of the gloom they all emerged, like a line of advancing soldiers. Her father, his face grim and angry. Her mother, worried. Nazeem, looking like a fierce little warrior. Miss Withers. Miss Withers? What was happening?

'You were all ready to get stuck right into her, weren't you? All of you against one little girl.' Miss Withers sounded disgusted. Then she added, 'I should have done something about this a long time ago.'

The two policemen were there too. Blue-eyes and Ginger.

Ivy stood rooted to the spot, too terrified, surprised, shocked, to move at all. The game, as they say, was definitely up.

Katie's mother ran to her and gathered her up in her arms. 'Oh, my wee darling, are you all right?'

Katie was puzzled. It was all like a dream. 'But . . . I don't understand.'

Nazeem bounded up to her enthusiastically. 'That was me. You see, at your house, I saw Ivy and all of them follow you when you ran off. They'd probably followed me and waited to see what you would do. I knew they were up to something, so I followed them. They led me here, and I knew you were in trouble, so I ran home to get your mum and dad.'

Her mother took up the story. 'I came in from the garden and you'd gone, and the door was wide open. I thought something terrible had happened. I called the police.'

'The police were there when I arrived,' Nazeem broke in. 'I told them everything . . . And so was Miss Withers.' Nazeem went on, as if the teacher's presence still baffled her.

'I was angry. You didn't come to school. Your parents didn't come to the meeting I'd arranged. So, after school, I decided to come to your house.' Miss Withers crouched down beside Katie and her mother. Her voice became soft, her eyes softer still. This was Miss Withers? 'I'm so glad I did.'

She looked at Ivy. 'When I think of what those girls were going to do to you . . .'

Her father leaned down to her. 'But Katie, why did you come to this awful place to begin with?'

Katie jumped to her feet. Zan! That should have been her first thought, but things were happening so fast.

'Zan! We've got to help her!' They all looked puzzled. Her parents, Miss Withers, Nazeem, even the police, already preparing to lead Ivy and co. off to their police car. Katie began to pull away from her mother.

'She does exist, Mum. And Whittaker is after her. Believe me. She didn't burn the house down. Whittaker did. Zan saw him do it, and he's been after her ever since.' She could see disbelief flit across their faces, but they had to believe her this time. They had to. 'Don't you see, Dad? That's why I couldn't tell anyone about her. She's been afraid of Whittaker . . . and now he's got her.' Suddenly, she remembered the terror in Zan's eyes. 'Please!' she screamed.

Her father glanced round at the police. 'Come on. Where did they go, Katie?'

She pointed at the warehouse. 'In there.'

They all ran, spreading out as they searched, only the moon darting in and out of clouds lighting their way until the policemen switched on their torches and two shafts of light weaved across their path. They would never find her, Katie thought. Perhaps she would never know what happened to Zan. She prayed again. Prayed for another miracle.

Blue-eyes beamed his light to the rafters above, and there, suddenly caught for a moment, were two figures.

'There!' Katie shouted, pulling at her father's sleeve. 'She's up there!'

Light from the two torches merged on the beam above. Everyone down below gasped. Zan was hanging by her fingers from one of those old creaky beams. It didn't look as if it was going to hold for long, and lying across it was Whittaker, his face in the torchlight more sinister than ever.

'My God, Douglas. Look what he's doing.'

Whittaker was trying to prise Zan's fingers from their hold, trying to make her lose her grip! Kate had never seen such determination on Zan's face. She would hold on. She must!

'We can see everything, Whittaker!' Blue-eyes called up to him. 'Leave the girl be.'

Taken by surprise, Whittaker slipped on the beam. In a second he had righted himself. He looked down. Saw them all, must have known he was done for. Then he balled his fist and brought it down viciously against Zan's fingers.

Zan yelled and that one hand lost its grip. Everyone below gasped again.

'Hold on, Zan!' Katie screamed up at her.

Whittaker started edging his way back along the beam.

'Let's get him,' Blue-eyes said, and without a moment's hesitation the policemen raced into the darkness. Katie grabbed her father tightly. 'Please, Dad. We've got to get Zan.'

Zan was holding on with one hand, biting her lip, her eyes clenched tight with determination.

'I'll get her,' Katie's father said.

Breathless, they watched as he climbed. Up the rickety old ladder to the platform where Zan had lived. Katie's eyes darted from her father to Zan. She must hold on. He must get to her in time! Zan's hand slipped just a fraction. Katie screamed. 'Hold on, just a wee while, Zan. Please!' Katie had never felt so helpless. Her father was astride the beam now, inching his way towards Zan. Katie could hear his soft words of comfort.

'Just you hold on. I'm coming. You'll be safe soon. Just a minute more. You can do it.'

But would Zan believe him? Would she trust him? Zan didn't even like her father!

Oh, Zan, trust him, please. He's wonderful. Just trust him!

Then he was beside her. He reached down, his hand held out to Zan, and grabbed her wrist. 'Give me your other hand,' he said. Zan would have to reach out to him now. He was leaning down as far as he could. Any more and he would fall himself.

Zan shook her head. 'I . . . can't . . .'

Everyone held their breath. Not a sound broke the ominous silence. Then the beam creaked. Her mother drew in a sharp breath. Miss Withers let out a scream.

'Give me your hand. Right now, Zan!!!!' Katie knew that tone of her father's. Obey me, or else. Zan recognized it too. She threw her hand up, and he grabbed it. With all his strength he pulled. Freeing his other hand, he grabbed her jacket and pulled hard until she could scramble on to the beam beside him. A cheer went up. Zan threw her arms round Katie's father. He hugged her close. Was Zan crying? Katie was certainly in tears.

'We're not out of the woods yet,' she heard her father say. 'Let's get off this beam.'

This time there was no inching along. Her father got to his feet, and pulled Zan to hers.

'How's your balance?' he asked her.

'Like a monkey!' she said at once.

'Come on then.' And together, hand in hand, they ran deftly along the beam to the platform.

The beam creaked again. Splinters of rotten wood began to fall from it. With one bound they jumped to the platform. Just in time.

'It's going!' Miss Withers screamed, waving everyone back. 'Get out of the way!' Katie's mother grabbed Katie and Nazeem and jerked them back from any danger. Katie saw Ivy throw herself to the ground screaming as the beam crashed to the floor.

Dust rose, splinters flew. Everyone began to cough.

It took a moment for it all to sink in. They were safe,

her father and Zan.

Nazeem was the first to jump excitedly in the air. She began dancing around, hugging Katie! 'They did it. They did it.' Miss Withers and her mother hugged each other. Katie ran to the ladder. Her father and Zan were already descending.

Zan stepped off first. She looked at Katie. They didn't say a word. They had proved a friendship beyond words. They smiled at each other, and suddenly they were hugging and crying and laughing, all at the same time. Her father stepped off the ladder. Katie ran to him now. She was so proud of him, she hugged him. Her mother ran and fell into their embrace. The three of them, a family, caring for each other. Zan took a step back.

It was Katie's father who noticed first. He held out an outstretched arm to Zan. She hesitated, but for only a second, then she moved into his arms. A quick hug was what she probably had in mind. But Zan didn't know her parents when they got started. Her mother joined in hugging Zan too, and Katie, never one to be left out, just held on tight. She could feel Zan shaking, the fear still upon her, and she could feel that fear abate as her father's strength, her family's strength, comforted her.

Zan – safe at last.

CHAPTER SIXTEEN

If only Zan could be with us for Christmas. She remembered the day she had thought that, hoped for it, prayed for it.

Now it was Christmas.

Christmas Day.

The house was gaily decorated, a welcoming fire burned in the hearth, the table looked beautiful with its red and white tablecloth and the green napkins arranged in sparkling wine glasses.

It should have been her best Christmas ever . . . Instead . . .

Katie sighed. She should be happy. Whittaker was safely behind bars awaiting trial. The proof of his villainy had been plain for all to see when he had tried to prise Zan's fingers from the beam that awful night. Zan was exonerated. Katie had heard that word a lot over the

177

past few weeks. Her innocence proved beyond doubt. It had long ago been discovered that her parents had links with a highly dangerous gang of criminals. The initial theory that Zan had to be responsible for the fire was eventually questioned when the truth about them came out. Zan had never known that, of course. Always on the run, with no reason to trust either the police or social workers, or parents for that matter.

She had trusted Katie's dad that day. And it had seemed natural and right for her to come home with them. At least until matters were sorted out.

Katie and Zan, together, at least for this Christmas!

Yet, here she was on Christmas Day . . . miserable! And it was all Zan's fault.

'Katie, are you coming to sit down? Or don't you want any Christmas dinner?'

Katie stuck her nose in the air and continued looking into the flames.

'She's still in a huff. Leave her be.'

Katie jumped from her seat. 'I'm in a huff, am I? And why am I in a huff?'

She looked at Zan . . . yes, Zan . . . and glowered.

Zan shrugged and looked faintly amused. 'So I used the last of the mousse. I'll get you more.'

'But it's Christmas Day. All the shops are closed. And just look at my hair.'

She was selfish! There was no other word for her!

'It looks lovely, dear. Now come and sit down,' her mother said.

'Not beside her!' And she and Zan nudged each other deliberately as they passed.

'Suits me,' Zan said.

'Next time, I'm buying my own mousse,' Katie said. 'And I'm writing my name all over it!'

Zan sat down and waved out her napkin and spread it on her knees. She had adapted well to family life, Katie thought. Sitting there, with her Christmas dress on, and her hair all cut and shiny . . . with *her* mousse!

'All of this over some silly hair mousse,' her mother complained.

'You went away with the last of the hairspray,' Zan retorted.

'She does it all the time, Mum!' Katie said. 'My mousse, my deodorant, my . . .'

Her mother touched her hand. 'Katie, I know it's hard for you to get used to sharing things.' She smiled at Zan and touched her hand too. 'And for you too, Zan. Neither of you have ever had to share things before.'

That wasn't going to win Katie over. 'Well, she's not getting a loan of any of my clothes again!'

'I hope you remember that tomorrow night,' Zan said smugly. 'Christmas disco. Remember? You asked if you could wear my green top.'

Katie was horrified. 'You promised I could have it! Mum, she promised!'

Suddenly, her mother banged the table with her fists, so hard that even her dad, who had been watching the proceedings with a fatherly, affectionate eye, jumped in his seat.

'That's it!' she shouted. 'I've had enough! It's Christmas Day! Zan's aunt will be here in a few days, and goodness knows when we'll see her again. So I want the Peace and Goodwill to start right now!'

Zan's aunt. Katie glanced at Zan guiltily. Zan couldn't stay with them. How hurt and angry Katie had been when she'd first heard. She'd dreamed of them both together for ever . . . like sisters. She saw, too, in Zan's bright eyes, apprehension. She didn't know this aunt. Coming all the way from Australia to claim her, care for her. An aunt who hadn't even known of Zan's existence till a couple of weeks ago. So far, all she had been to Zan was a sympathetic letter, a tearful voice on the phone.

Zan's mother's youngest sister, who had tried to escape the family's violence, just as Zan had. A kindred spirit? Katie hoped she was.

'Oh well,' Zan had said when she knew there was no alternative. 'It'll be an adventure.'

Life with Zan, Katie thought, always would be.

Zan wanted to stay here too. Katie knew that. But it was not to be. Except for this Christmas. And here she was spoiling it, all for the sake of some silly mousse. Zan looked up at her, the same thoughts in her mind. She shrugged. 'Have the top,' she said.

Katie smiled back.

Her father sighed. 'Ah, they're smiling, Katherine. Thank heaven for that. I thought for a minute they weren't going to eat this turkey. They were going to throw it at each other.'

Zan began to laugh, and so did Katie. And soon they were all laughing.

'I'd like to propose a toast,' her father said, and he held his glass high. 'To Katie and Zan . . .' He smiled at each of them. 'Friends for ever.'

Who knew what the future held for both of them? All Katie knew now was that they would always be friends. An adventure behind them. Who was to say how many more in front of them? They would be together again. She just knew it. They'd never be far apart.

They clinked their glasses across the table. They didn't have to say a word. Each knew what the other was thinking.

Friends for ever.

Loved *Run Zan Run*?

**Then turn the page to find out about Cathy MacPhail
and her inspiration for this gripping story**

Why I wrote *Run Zan Run*

Run Zan Run is the book that changed my life. I had no intention of ever writing young teenage fiction. I thought I was going to be a comedy scriptwriter – I had two series on the radio and was having scripts developed for television. Then one night when my daughter, Katie, was on the way to the school youth club she was attacked by a gang of boys and girls, a lot older than her, a gang who had a bad reputation both in and out of school.

It was after that the real bullying started. Katie couldn't walk along the school corridors or go beyond the school gates without them waiting for her. She hated going to school and so I wanted her to move to another school, but Katie wanted to stay where she was. What happened to Katie made me see how often teachers' hands are tied when dealing with bullies. I was growing angrier and feeling more and more useless. Finally, I decided I was going to write a book about it. But I knew right then that I didn't just want to write a book about bullying, I wanted to write the kind of book

I like to read – a mystery and a thriller. I wanted it to have cliffhangers and build to an exciting climax. Most of all, I wanted someone in the book to help Katie because no one was helping her in real life. And that was how Zan was born. Do you know what Zan is short for? I do tell you in the book. We never do find out her real name. I love putting unsolved mysteries in my books – they make you think. The original title for *Run Zan Run* was 'The Girl in the Cardboard Box'. Do you think 'Run Zan Run' is better? My editor told me that to have an active verb in the title gives the book a sense of pace. I have never forgotten that advice.

I have now written over thirty books and I don't think I would have written any of them if that awful thing hadn't happened to Katie. Isn't it amazing how one thing can change your life. I have told Katie that it might have been the worst thing that ever happened to her but it was the best thing that ever happened to me . . . and she just shakes her head and says 'Mum, you're a sick woman.'

Meet Cathy MacPhail

Cathy MacPhail was born and brought up in Greenock, Scotland, where she still lives. Before becoming a children's author, she wrote short stories for magazines and comedy programmes for radio. Cathy was inspired to write her first children's book after her daughter was bullied at school.

Cathy writes spooky thrillers for younger readers as well as teen novels. She has won the Royal Mail Book Award twice, along with lots of other awards. She loves to give her readers a 'rattling good read' and has been called the Scottish Jacqueline Wilson.

One of Cathy's greatest fears would be to meet another version of herself, similar to the young girl in her bestselling novel *Another Me*. She is a big fan of *Doctor Who* and would love to write a scary monster episode for the series.

Cathy loves to hear from her fans, so visit **www.cathymacphail.com** and email her your thoughts.

Q&A with Cathy MacPhail

What are your favourite things to do when you're not writing?

When I'm not writing, I'm usually reading or visiting family – I love spending time with my children, turning up on their doorsteps when they least expect me! I enjoy going on cruises too because it's the perfect way for me to visit new places. Like most people, I also love going to the cinema. I always have done.

What are your favourite films?

Oh, there are so many films I love. *It's a Wonderful Life* is one of them. The hero is an ordinary man with just a few problems that are getting him down. Then he is visited by an angel who shows him how life would have been if he had never been born and he realises that his life is worthwhile after all.

Another fantastic film is *The Searchers*. A story set in America in the mid nineteenth-century about a man's struggle to find his niece who has been kidnapped by the Sioux. It explores issues of racism that were common at the time.

But at the top of my list is *Some Like It Hot*. Two men pretend to be female musicians to escape gangsters and one of them falls in love with Marilyn Monroe! It's so funny and it has the best last line of any film I've ever seen, 'Oh well, nobody's perfect.'

If you could be a character from a book, who would you be?

I have thought and thought about this because most books I've read have at least one wonderful character that I'd like to be, but I think Elizabeth Bennet has to be my first pick. She is so bright. Then there's Cathy from *Wuthering Heights*. I like her passionate nature, and we share a first name! Also, both of them are admired by fantastic men! When I'm really old, I want to be Miss Marple. I will go around annoying people and solving murders.

Did I ever write stories at school?

I wrote stories all the time. I loved it when the teacher said we were going to write a story. Mine were always about beautiful Scottish girls, usually with long, red hair, who travelled the world and had adventures with handsome cowboys, Arab sheiks or titled English noblemen. I wasn't interested in gritty reality and who, I thought, would want to read a story about a wee girl who lived with her mother and three sisters in a tenement flat in Greenock, Scotland. It took me a long time to appreciate the stories that you can find in real life.

Cathy's Choice

My Three Favourite Books as a Child

Little Women, by Lousia May Alcott, is about four sisters and one of them wants to be a writer. I was one of four sisters and I dreamed of one day being a writer.

Pride and Prejudice, by Jane Austen, has to be one of my top three books. This book is about sisters and their relationships with each other. Every time I read it I find something else I enjoy about it, whether it is the witty dialogue, the humour or the wonderful characters – and there are so many besides Mr Darcy and Elizabeth Bennet.

The Pears' Cyclopaedia (No, honestly!). I got this as a gift for my tenth birthday and it contained so much information about everything that I was always reading it. I still find things in it that help me with my writing.